WITHDRAWN

W9-BZV-677

The Sky Is Falling

Kit Pearson

WITHDRAWN

VIKING
KESTREL

VIKING KESTREL

Published by the Penguin Group
Penguin Books Canada Ltd, 10 Alcorn Avenue, Toronto, Ontario, Canada
M4V 3B2
Penguin Books Ltd, 27 Wrights Lane, London W8 5TZ, England
Viking Penguin, a division of Penguin Books USA Inc., 375 Hudson Street,
New York, New York 10014, USA
Penguin Books Australia Ltd, Ringwood, Victoria, Australia
Penguin Books (NZ) Ltd, 182-190 Wairau Road, Auckland 10,
New Zealand

Penguin Books Ltd, Registered Offices: Harmondsworth, Middlesex,
England

First published in 1989

5 7 9 10 8 6 4

Copyright © Kathleen Pearson, 1989

All rights reserved. Without limiting the rights under copyright reserved
above, no part of this publication may be reproduced, stored in or
introduced into a retrieval system, or transmitted in any form or by any
means (elctronic, mechanical, photocopying, recording or otherwise),
without the prior written permission of both the copyright owner and the
above publisher of this book.

*Publisher's note: This book is a work of fiction. Names, characters, places
and incidents either are the product of the author's imagination or are used
fictitiously, and any resemblance to actual persons living or dead, events,
or locales is entirely coincidental.*

Printed and bound in the United States of America

Canadian Cataloguing in Publication Data
Pearson, Kit, 1947-   The sky is falling
ISBN 0-670-82849-1
I. Title.
PS8581.E27S5 1989   JC813'54   C89-094231-5
PZ7.P42SK 1989

British Library Cataloguing in Publication Data Available
American Library of Congress Cataloguing in Publication Data Available

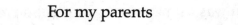
For my parents

It was a long journey they set out on,
and they did not think of any end to it . . .

"Alenoushka and Her Brother"
(Russian folk tale)

Contents

Part One

Part Two

Part Three

Part One

I

The Plane

Norah, armed to the teeth, slithered on her stomach through the underbrush. She gripped her bow in her right hand and bit on a kitchen knife. A quiver of arrows made from sharpened twigs and decorated with chicken feathers slid sideways on her back, getting tangled with the string of her gas mask case. Pulling herself forward by her elbows, she finally reached the clearing.

There she stopped to wait for Tom's signal. The knife had an unpleasantly metallic taste. Spitting it out, she looked up and gaped in wonder.

In front of her, glittering in the August sunlight, was a shot-down German aeroplane — a Messerschmitt 109. Norah recognized its square-cut wing tips and streamlined fuselage. But it looked more like a squashed dragonfly than a plane. Its wings stretched lifelessly over the ground and its split body exposed its innards. One propeller blade was bent back and twisted. Bullet holes spotted the metal corpse and a burnt, sour smell like vinegar rose from it.

The mangled machine looked alien and out of place in Mr Coomber's peaceful field. Most sinister of all was the bold black swastika on the plane's tail. When the war had begun a year ago, the Nazis had been safely on the other side of the Channel. Then they had started flying over England. And now, here was one of their planes only a few hundred yards away. A choking fear filled Norah, as if there were a weight on her chest.

She took a deep breath and pulled herself to a sitting position, careful to stay concealed. In front of the aircraft, puffed with importance, stood Mr Willis from the village, his crisp new Home Guard emblem around his sleeve.

Across the field, Tom waved his arm. Norah waved back and watched the answering signals from Harry and Jasper. Tom pointed to Norah. Good, they were going to assemble here. Maybe if she weren't alone this strange new fear would leave her.

"Isn't it *smashing*?" whispered Tom a few minutes later. He and the younger two crept up to join her, dropping their weapons.

With three warm bodies pressing close to hers, Norah breathed easily again. They all stared greedily at the plane's parts: its instrument panel, machine guns, fuel caps and hanging shards of aluminum. Harry and Jasper were too awed to speak.

"The tailfin's completely undamaged," said Tom softly. "If only Mr Willis wasn't there and we had a hacksaw, we could cut it off."

Several older boys broke through the trees on the opposite side of the field and hurried towards the plane, halting with frustration when they saw Mr Willis.

"Get away!" he called. "This plane will be guarded until the lorry comes, so there's no use hanging about."

One of the boys darted behind the plane, snatched up some metal from the ground and bolted with his companions. Mr Willis shouted helplessly after them.

"I wonder where the pilot is?" mused Tom. "See his gear?" He pointed to the parachute pack, leather helmet and goggles abandoned in front of the wreck. "He could be lurking somewhere!"

Norah had trouble breathing again as she took this in. One of Hitler's men! The Enemy, the Hun, who wanted to conquer Britain, except Britain would never give up.

"He'll probably surrender," said Tom, "or they'll capture him. Or *we* will," he added. Norah glanced doubtfully at her fragile arrows and the dull knife lying in the dirt.

They watched the plane for an hour, until their arms and legs were cramped and Jasper complained he was thirsty. Finally, when it became obvious that Mr Willis was not going to leave his post, they crept through the trees to their waiting bicycles. Slowly they rode back to Ringden, squeezing through the side of the barbed-wire roadblock. The guards knew them well and didn't bother asking for their identity cards.

As they neared the edge of the village, they waved to old Mrs Chandler, who had had her noon meal in her front garden every day this week so she could watch the fighting planes in the sky. They parked their bicycles and crossed the lumpy grass behind her house to their tree fort.

Tom handed around weak lemonade. The four children sat in companionable, exhausted silence, each intoxicated with the thrilling danger of the plane.

II

The Skywatchers

Old Mrs Chandler didn't know there was a secret society in her orchard. Her house was the largest and highest in Ringden and looked out over the Weald. Last summer Tom and Norah had discovered the old tree fort hidden in an apple tree; it must have been built by one of her sons. They had reinforced it with scraps of wood and added a rope ladder to get in and out quickly.

At first, the fort had been a good place in which to play Cops and Robbers. But this spring it had been named the Lookout when the Secret Society of Skywatchers was formed. Now they were on the alert for real enemies: the Good Guys were the English and the Bad Guys the Germans.

Pinned on the walls of the Lookout were pictures cut out of the newspaper of the troop-carrying aircraft to look out for. They especially hoped to catch sight of a Junkers 52, the enemy plane most commonly used for parachute dropping. They owned a copy of *Friend or Foe? A Young Spotter's Guide to Allied and German Aircraft*, but Tom and Norah were such experts, they no longer needed it.

The Skywatchers looked at strangers suspiciously and longed to meet nuns, monks or nurses who might be Nazis in disguise with collapsible bicycles under their loose clothes. In the Lookout was a supply of grey, lumpy sugar, painstakingly saved from their rations, to pour into enemies' petrol tanks and neutralize them.

Norah sipped her sour lemonade and looked around the cluttered fort with satisfaction. Ranged along a shelf were their war souvenirs: twisted bits of shrapnel, uniform badges and tins of cartridge cases. It was too bad they hadn't been able to get anything new from the Messerschmitt.

A government leaflet was attached to the tree trunk: "If the Invader Comes". Her eyes focused on the words, "If you run away . . . you will be machine-gunned from the air." Again, Norah felt as if there were a weight on her chest.

"Whose turn is it to keep watch?" asked Harry.

"Mine," said Norah, glad of a diversion. She squatted on the edge of the Lookout, pressing her father's old field glasses to her eyes. They were so heavy they made her arms ache, and after a few seconds she put them down and scanned the sky and landscape without them.

Below her stretched the rolling Weald, dotted with sheep and the gleaming white caps of oast houses. She could just glimpse where the land levelled off, like the edge of a table, as it dropped to Romney Marsh. Beyond that was the Channel and from across the Channel the Germans came . . . . West of the Lookout was the village, its stubby church spire poking up past the rooftops. Norah could even see her own house and her brother Gavin playing with his wagon in the garden.

She stared so intently at the dazzling sky that her eyes watered. Never before had the weather been as consistently clear as in this summer of 1940. "Hitler and the rain will come together," the grown-ups predicted.

Then, for the last month things had been falling out of the sky: stray bombs meant for the coast or the airfields; German propaganda leaflets that ended up being sold at raffles; and distant, floating parachutes like tiny puffballs. During the air battles, showers of empty cartridge cases tinkled on the roofs of Ringden; last week one had splashed into Mr Skinner's bucket as he was milking.

Yesterday a pilot's boot had plummeted into the grass behind the Lookout: a worn, black leather boot with the imprint of a man's big toe creasing the top. They were certain it was a Nazi boot, and it now had the place of honour in their collection.

Every day this week they had seen dogfights, as the clean sky became covered with a cobweb of the tangled white contrails of fighting planes. This morning's battle had been the most exciting. The planes had come lower than usual, and they could pick out the tiny, silvery Messerschmitts circling protectively around the moth-like Dorniers. Then they had heard the growl of RAF fighters tearing in to give battle. For once they were Spitfires instead of the more familiar, humpbacked Hurricanes. The graceful Spits had tilted and twisted, machine-gun fire had sounded faintly and the children had cheered so wildly they'd almost pushed each other off the platform.

That was when one of the German planes had dropped through the blueness. The Skywatchers had scrambled to their bicycles, but it had taken hours to find it. While they'd paused to eat their sandwiches, a passing boy had told them the plane was in a field at Mr Coomber's farm.

There was no more activity now. The only sound was the purr of threshing machines and the raspy quarrelling of rooks. The countryside had been prac- tically empty of cars since gas rationing, and the church bells would not ring again unless there was an invasion. Norah's eyes kept closing as she tried to concentrate on the sky. She was glad when her time was up and Harry took her place.

Behind her, the others had been reading comics and mending their bows. "We should write to Pete and Molly and tell them about the plane," said Norah. The Kemps had been active Skywatchers until, along with several other members, they'd been evacuated to Wales. Norah missed Molly; she had been her best friend. Now she supposed Tom was, although he was sometimes bossier than she liked.

"It would be better not to tell them," said Tom. "It'll just make them angry to know what they've missed."

"The Smiths are being sent away, too," Jasper said. "To Canada! My mum heard from their mum this morning."

"Canada?" Norah sputtered. She took down the Boot and examined it again, trying not to listen.

Tom looked disgusted. "Anyone who leaves England is a coward," he declared. "Derek and Dulcie and Lucy are so feeble, they probably *want* to go."

Harry turned around from his post. "Mum and Dad thought Jasper and me might go to our auntie's in Devon if the bombing starts. Now they've changed their minds, because it's just as dangerous there."

"*My* mum says that no place is safe, so her and me may as well stick it out together," boasted Tom. "She wouldn't even *consider* sending me away. And Norah's parents wouldn't either. We're lucky!"

"I'm going to fetch some water," said Norah abruptly, climbing down with the pail. She wove through trees heavy with ripening apples to the stream at the end of the orchard, thinking of everyone in Britain scurrying around like ants under a large, descending boot like theirs, all trying to find a safe place when there wasn't one.

She sat down by the water, took off her socks and shoes, and dangled her hot feet in the stream. She would linger here until they'd had time to finish talking about being sent away. For a few seconds the fleeting blue of a kingfisher distracted her. But she couldn't help brooding about evacuation.

Last fall her village had been considered safe. Hundreds of London children had been sent to the

Ashford area, and one whole school had come to Ringden. They boarded with different families and had their own classes in the church hall. For four months the 'vaccies and the village children had waged a battle of hurled mud and words. The visitors complained about having to go all the way into Gilden to see the pictures; the village mothers objected to the bad language their children were learning. When nothing seemed to be happening in the war, the evacuees had returned to London.

But then the "phoney war" had ended and the danger had become real. When France fell and Churchill said the Battle of Britain had begun, Norah had helped pull up all the signposts in the village to confuse the enemy. "We shall fight in the field and in the streets, we shall fight in the hills," Churchill's solemn voice chanted from the wireless.

Norah was proud that her whole family was helping to fight. In January her older sisters, Muriel and Tibby, had joined the Auxiliary Territorial Service; they were stationed in Chester. "Not a nice thing for young girls, being in the forces like a man," said nosy Mrs Curteis next door. But Dad was proud. "My girls are as brave as any man," he boasted. He was too old to enlist, so he joined the Home Guard. Mum spent every morning in the church hall, marking blankets and sewing hospital bags for wounded soldiers. Norah, besides performing her Skywatcher duties, had donated sixpence to the village Spitfire fund — enough to manufacture one rivet. Gavin wasn't doing anything, but he was only five — too young and silly to count.

The war was the most exciting thing that had ever happened in Norah's ten years, and this summer was the best part of it. Other summers were a pleasant, mild blur of building sandcastles on the beach near Grandad's house in Camber. But one day at the end of last August, Norah had found herself filling sandbags instead of playing.

Now there was a bright edge to everything; even the weather was exaggerated. The coldest winter in a hundred years was followed by a short spring and an early summer. As the war news grew worse and the grown-ups huddled anxiously around the wireless, day after day dawned hot and clear. At night, the sky's inky blackness was pinpointed with strangely brilliant stars, the only lights in Britain besides the searchlights that were not blacked out.

Every evening this week the news announcer had given out the "scores" of the battle in the sky as if it were a football match. Norah could hardly remember what life had been like before this war. How could anyone bear to be sent away from it? Tom was right — they were lucky that their parents were so sensible.

But then she felt afraid again, because she wasn't at all sure that *her* parents would remain sensible.

III

Little Whitebull

After Norah had run back to the fort and swished out the lemonade cups, they all started home for tea. When they reached the middle of the village, Harry and Jasper gave the Skywatchers' secret signal — little finger and thumb extended like an aeroplane — and scampered down their lane. Tom and Norah put their fingers crossways under their noses and goose-stepped down the main street, singing loudly in time:

> Whistle while you work!
> Mussolini is a twerp!
> Hitler's barmy
> So's his army
> Whistle while you work!

They passed the church and the stone vicarage beside it. The Smiths were probably inside, packing to go to Canada. Dulcie was in Norah's class. She was the sort of girl who fretted if she forgot her handkerchief. Lucy was a little older than Gavin and spent a lot of her time whining.

"Poor Goosey and Loosey," mocked Norah. "I bet they'll be afraid of wolves in Canada." Being nasty helped her calm down a bit. Then she felt sorry for them — they would be left out of the war.

She said goodbye to Tom at his mother's grocery shop and ran to her house. She was late for tea, but Mum probably wouldn't scold her.

That was part of Norah's increasing uneasiness. Her parents let her and Gavin stay up late, spoke to them in strange, gentle voices and gave them sad looks when they thought the children didn't notice. Gavin probably didn't. But every night Norah listened to Mum and Dad's worried murmur downstairs.

Norah paused at the front of her small, weatherboarded house. Its shabby exterior was brightened by the masses of zinnias and hollyhocks that flanked the door. A sign on the sagging gate said Little Whitebull in faded wooden letters. No one knew why their house was called that. It had been already named when her parents had bought it, just after Muriel was born.

The gate needed painting as well as mending, but Dad was too busy these days to do much work around the house. Norah studied the loose hinges; perhaps she could fix it and show them how useful she was. She could paint the sign again in bright red. And she would start to keep her room tidier and help with the washing up. Feeling more cheerful, she ran into the house.

"I'm home!" she shouted, clattering through the front room to the large kitchen where they spent most of their time. "Sorry I'm late, Mum."

Mrs Stoakes came out of the scullery and wiped back the lank hair that always hung into her eyes. "Where have you *been*, Norah?" she asked anxiously. "You weren't anywhere near that German plane, were you? I just heard about it."

"Not really," mumbled Norah. Not near enough to touch it, she added to herself.

Her mother shuddered. "It was terribly close. The next thing we know, we'll have one on top of us. Sit down, sweetheart, there's sausages."

Sweetheart? Mum never gushed; she was usually quick tempered and brusque. Now she was like a person in disguise.

If she was going to play-act, then Norah would too. "Thanks, Mum," she said politely. "Did you have to queue long at the butcher's?" She forced herself to eat slowly instead of wolfing down her food as usual.

Gavin was the only person who was himself. He sat at the table with his jammy bread divided into two, marching each one to collide with its twin and come apart in sticky strings. He hummed to himself with a dreamy expression, the way he always did in his private games.

Norah glanced at her mother. Surely she'd have to react to such a mess: there was jam all over the tablecloth. But all Mum said was, "Here, pet, let me wipe your hands."

Norah sighed. Gavin usually got away with a lot,

but not sloppy eating. She bent over her milky tea, her brain buzzing. Something was definitely up.

The hens in the back garden chittered indignantly as Dad pushed through the scullery door. He removed the bicycle clips from his trouser legs, kissed Mum, ruffled Gavin's hair and grinned at Norah. "What have *you* been up to today? Seen anything interesting?" His green-grey eyes, which everyone said were exactly like hers, teased her as usual.

Norah forgot to be polite. "Oh, Dad, there was a crash-landed plane — a ME 109! You could see the bullet holes and the swastika and everything!"

"I passed it on my way home — the lorry was taking it away."

"Norah!" snapped Mum. "I thought you said you weren't close! You have to be more careful or I'll make you stay in your own garden, like the Smith girls. I really don't know what to do with you these days — the war is making you wild."

"Now, Jane, she couldn't come to much harm looking at a plane that's out of commission," said Dad mildly.

This was more normal. Norah relaxed and concentrated on her sausages, as Dad collapsed in his favourite chair with a groan. "Come and pull my shoes off, old man," he said to Gavin. He had only an hour between arriving home from his bookkeeping job in Gilden and setting out for his Home Guard duties.

Gavin picked up his small worn elephant and went over to his father. "Creature will pull your shoes off — he's very strong."

What a baby Gavin was, still playing with toy animals. Jasper was only three years older, but he was as brave as Tom. Gavin was such a namby-pamby brother. Everyone said he should have been a girl, and Norah a boy.

Dad looked up from the pages of the *Kentish Express*. "They're letting the hop-pickers come from London as usual," he said to Mum. "It says arrangements have been made for protection in case of air raids."

Mum opened the scullery door to cool off the steamy kitchen, which smelled pleasantly of hot fat and the clean clothes airing in front of the grate. Dad switched on the wireless and Gavin curled up in his lap. The familiar voice of Larry the Lamb filled the room.

Norah pretended to be too old for "The Children's Hour", but she still liked hearing Dennis the Dachshund talk backwards. As she listened, she surprised her mother by first helping dry the dishes and then sitting down to struggle with her knitting. The oily grey wool, which was supposed to be turned into a "comfort" for a sailor, cut into her hands.

"Good-night, children, everywhere," said the voice from the wireless.

"Good-night, Uncle Mac," said Gavin solemnly, as he always did.

"Dad," whispered Norah nervously, after the news was over and while Mum was still in the scullery. There was something she had to find out, even though it scared her to ask. "Do you know if they found the pilot?"

Dad gave her a warning glance, the one that meant Don't Worry Your Mother. "Yes," he murmured. "They picked him up near Woodchurch. He was wounded, poor lad — gave himself up easily."

Norah's chest felt lighter. At least she didn't have to worry about him wandering into their village.

Of course, if Hitler invaded Britain, as everyone thought he might, a *lot* of Nazis might come into Ringden — even into Little Whitebull! That thought made Norah feel choked up again and she shifted irritably. What was the matter with her? She had never been afraid before.

Her father stood up and stretched. "Time to get changed." He caught his wife's eye before he added, "Don't make any plans for the morning, Norah. Your mother and I want to discuss something with you. And I'll help you finish your kite tomorrow, Gavin, since it's Saturday."

"Can I stay up and listen to TTMA?" Norah asked desperately. If he said no, everything would be ordinary.

"I don't see why not," said Dad gently.

After he left, dressed in his World War I uniform and carrying a shotgun, Norah made herself into a tight ball in his chair. Her suspicions were growing to a terrible certainty.

Before she had time to ponder further, the back door opened again and a tubby man with a snowy fringe around his otherwise bald head struggled in, loaded with packages and suitcases.

"Grandad!" shouted Norah and Gavin.

"Father! What on earth are *you* doing here?"

The old man chuckled as he let his luggage drop. He lifted Gavin into the air. "Bombed out! The dratted Hun put one right through my roof! All rubble, my dears, all rubble. So I've come to stay with you." He bent over to Norah and tickled her cheek with his stiff moustache. "What do you think of that, my fierce little soldier?"

Mum sank to a chair. "Bombed out . . . Father, are you all right? Are you hurt?"

"Don't fret, Janie. I'm right as rain, because I wasn't at home when they called. Came back from the pub to find a flattened house. So I just packed up what I could find and got on the bus. Better to live inland anyhow — the salt air was bad for my rheumatism." His sea-blue eyes sparkled under his droopy white eyebrows. "Got enough room for your old dad?"

"You know we have — we'd always give you a home. But you could have been killed! Oh, Father, this bloody war . . . "

Norah froze, shocked, as her mother, whom she had never seen cry, began to shake with sobs. Her mouth trembled and the tears slid over her thin cheeks as her weeping grew louder.

"*Don't*, Muv!" cried Gavin, pulling on her arm. "Did you hurt yourself?" Mrs Stoakes pulled him onto her knee and clutched him to her, burying her face in his neck. Gavin looked scared and tried to free himself.

"Now, now, Jane, enough of that." Grandad patted his daughter's shoulder awkwardly. "I *wasn't* killed. Never felt more alive, in fact. Nothing like a close call to make you see things in perspective! We'll weather this war out together now — that's how it should be, the whole family in one place." He released Gavin from his mother's grasp. "If you search my pockets, you might find a sweetie."

To avoid watching her mother, Norah turned to the fire and lifted the heavy kettle of water onto the grate. She had never made tea on her own before, but she'd seen Mum do it often enough. When the water boiled she poured it carefully over the leaves and filled the cups with milk, sugar and tea. She offered one to Mum and one to Grandad.

"Norah, what a help!" Mum's tears had stopped and she gave a weak smile. "What would I do without you?" Then she looked as if she might cry again.

Norah poured herself a cup, surprised her mother hadn't said anything about using some of tomorrow's rations. They all sat around the kitchen table and, to her relief, the adults began to talk normally.

Norah stared incredulously at Grandad, hardly daring to believe he was here. The war was shifting people around too rapidly. Some, like Molly and Muriel and Tibby, suddenly went away; others turned up unannounced and homeless. A few days ago the whole of Mrs Parker's brother's large family had arrived on her doorstep. Their house in Detling had been bombed and they, too, had been lucky enough to be out when it happened.

Norah's throat and chest constricted with fear as she thought of Grandad's cottage, the one where she'd spent her summers, flattened to rubble. But Grandad

was safe, and it would be wonderful to have him living
with them. She wondered what Dad would think.
Although Mum and Grandad often argued, they
thrived on it. Dad was always polite, but Norah knew
he and the old man didn't agree on much.

Grandad winked at Norah. "Now we'll have a
good time, eh young ones?"

Norah winked back. She climbed onto Grandad's
knee and began to tell him about the plane.

Later that night a commotion downstairs woke her
up. Dad had arrived home and was exclaiming about
finding Grandad there. Norah lay rigidly in bed, listening to the usual murmur of worried adult voices. Then
Grandad's rose above the rest, angry and accusing. She
couldn't make out his words but the stubborn strength
in his voice cheered her up. If her parents were telling
him the decision she dreaded, Grandad was on her
side.

IV

"I Won't Go!"

They told her after breakfast. Mum had sent Gavin over to play with Joey, who lived across the road. Norah was dismayed when Grandad went out as well, a furious expression on his face.

She was invited to sit down in the front room. Muriel insisted on calling it the "drawing room". It was only used on special occasions — when Muriel and Tibby entertained their young men, or when the vicar came to tea. The flimsy chairs were too stiff to be comfortable, as if they proclaimed "only serious matters are discussed here."

Norah tipped back her chair and waited. Mum had just polished the windows and a faint whiff of ammonia came from them. For the rest of her life, Norah would never smell ammonia without a flutter of panic.

Dad began speaking in such a cheerful voice that she wanted to scream. "Well, Norah, you and Gavin are going to have a great adventure!"

"No —" said Norah at once, but he waved her to be still. "Hold your horses! Just listen for a moment, then you can have your say. You're going to travel on a big ship . . . all the way to Canada! Canadian families have offered to provide homes for British children until the war is over. Your mother and I would feel much more at ease if we knew you and Gavin were safe. And what an opportunity for you, to go overseas, to learn about another country . . . "

His voice faltered at Norah's expression. Mum looked as stricken as she was.

"I know it's upsetting," Dad continued gently, "but I think you knew we were considering it."

Of course she had known. After France had fallen in June, all the grown-ups had talked about sending the children away. That was when Molly and Pete had gone. She'd heard Dad read aloud the newspaper notice about applying for overseas evacuation, but she was too worried to ask if they'd actually done it. A few days later Dad had asked casually, "Norah, if you could visit another country, which one would you prefer — Australia, New Zealand, South Africa, or Canada . . . "

"None of them!" Norah had cried.

Then Norah and Gavin had had their photographs taken in Gilden. Norah had wondered why.

But after that, for a long time, nothing more had been said. She had almost forgotten about it in the growing excitement of the war. The possibility of being sent away had festered under the surface, however, and now at last it had burst open like a ripe boil. For a few seconds Norah sat in stunned disbelief. Then she jumped up, knocking over her chair.

"I won't go!"

"Calm down," said Dad. He reached out his arm, but Norah brushed it aside. Dad sighed. "Listen to me, Norah. You've had an easy, sheltered life up to now. Now we're asking you to do something difficult. I know you can — you've always been my bravest girl."

"But I don't *want* to!" She was astounded that they would force her. "I don't want to go away to another country and leave you! I'd miss you! I'd miss out on the war! It's braver to stay here, not to run away! And children are *useful*. I watch for paratroopers every day, just like the Observer Corps. I helped pull up the signposts. And I'll do some of the housework so Mum can spend more time at the hall. I'll think of something for Gavin to do, too. I'll — I'll teach him to knit!"

Mum looked close to tears again. "Oh Norah, Norah, of course you don't want to go. I wish so much you didn't have to. But don't you see how going would be helping the war? You'd free Dad and me from worrying about you. And . . . " She paused, as if she weren't sure she should go on, "and if worse comes to worse, at least two members of the family will be safe and . . . free."

"And you'll be like ambassadors!" broke in Dad. "You'll meet children from another country and promote international understanding. That's the best way I can think of to end war . . . "

"Have you told her?" Grandad stood in the doorway, wiping his shining forehead with his handkerchief.

Mum turned to him impatiently. "Father, we said we wanted to be alone with Norah! Yes, we've told her — but we haven't finished. Please wait until we have."

But Grandad came into the room, muttering, "I'm part of this family too." He pulled Norah onto his knee and Norah's spirits lifted. Just in time!

With an irritated glance at Grandad, Dad continued to explain to Norah why it would be safer if she and Gavin left England.

"What will *Hitler* think if we start fleeing the country?" interrupted Grandad. "We're supposed to be sticking together and fighting!"

"Norah and Gavin are only children," said Dad patiently.

"Then what will he think about us panicking so much that we send away our children? I suppose you'll send *me* next! Get rid of the young and the old! We're useless, so send us away!"

"Father!" Mum turned bright pink. "They're our children — let *us* decide, and stop interfering. If you can't keep quiet, then leave the room."

Grandad scowled at her, but he shut up. He and Norah listened to the rest of Mum and Dad's reasonable arguments. And, slowly, Norah realized that they had lost. Grown-ups could always make children do what they wanted them to. She felt Grandad give a long sigh. Old people had to do what grown-ups decided, too.

Norah slid down to the floor, drew her feet up and clutched her knees to her chest. Her eyes prickled but she forced them wide open — she would *not* cry .

Desperately, she tried one last argument. "Even the princesses aren't being evacuated!" she protested. "The Queen said in the paper that they wouldn't send them out of the country — Tom's mum read it to us." Norah had always felt a special link with Princess Margaret Rose, who was almost her age. She was sure Margaret Rose had refused to go, and that's what had convinced the King and Queen.

But Mum and Dad just smiled, the way they did when they thought Norah was being amusing. "The princesses are in a safe part of the country somewhere, not right in the path of an invasion as you are," said Dad. "And a large number of well-off children *have* been sent overseas. Why should they be the only ones? Now the government has finally decided to pay for those who can't afford it."

Norah felt small and lost and wounded.

"You must have some questions," Dad prompted.

"When do we go?" she asked weakly.

"On Monday. Mum will take you to London, and an escort will meet you there. I wish it wasn't so sudden, but they only let us know a few days ago."

"There will be lots of other children with you," said Mum. "It will be like a church picnic! And the Smiths are going too, so you'll have someone from your own village along. Derek can keep an eye on all of you."

"Where — where shall we *live* in Canada? How

long will we have to stay?"

"You'll be living somewhere in Ontario," Dad told her. "I believe it's the largest province. You won't know who you'll be staying with until you get there, but I'm sure they'll be good people. Anyone who offers to do this must be kind. And we don't know for how long . . . " He looked apologetic. "Perhaps a year."

A *year*? When they came home she would be eleven! And leaving the day after *tomorrow*?

Dad was watching her. "Norah, I think that's enough to absorb for now. You go out and play and we'll talk about it again later. Send Gavin home, will you? I don't know how much he'll understand, but he has to be told."

As Norah left, her parents were arguing with Grandad again, but his voice sounded old and defeated. It was no use. They were sending her away and there was nothing she could do about it.

V

Too Many Goodbyes

"But you *can't!*" Tom cried.

"I have to. I told them all the reasons they shouldn't send me, but they don't understand."

The four Skywatchers sat in gloomy silence. They were used to grown-ups not understanding.

"Do you — do you think I'm a coward?" Norah asked Tom. She couldn't bear it if he did.

"Of course not — you don't want to go. But it's a rotten shame." Tom glanced at the two wide-eyed little boys. He looked deflated. "Everyone's leaving! First Pete and Molly and the Fowlers, and now you. How are we going to keep up our work with just three of us?"

They sat in a row without speaking, watching the sky as usual. But there had been no battles today and the air was ominously still, as if the war had stopped to hold its breath.

Norah already felt like a stranger. "Can I pick some shrapnel to take?" she asked finally.

Tom nodded and she chose some jagged pieces from their collection. She yearned for the Boot, but it was much too big to pack, and it belonged in the Lookout.

"You can have the plane book if you like," said Tom.

"What for?" said Norah. "There won't be any enemy planes flying over Canada — there's no war there." A country without a war seemed a very dull prospect.

Then the goodbyes began. Dad sent a telegram to Muriel and Tibby and they returned one immediately. HAVE WONDERFUL TIME KEEP CHEERFUL it said, as if Norah and Gavin were going on a holiday. It was so long since the older girls had left Ringden that receiving a farewell message seemed unnecessary; Norah had *said* goodbye to them.

That afternoon the friends and neighbours Norah had known all her life began dropping in with advice.

"I've given your mother some of my camomile tea," said Mrs Curteis. "If you sip some every morning until you board the ship, you won't be seasick."

"Aren't you a lucky girl, to see the world!" said Norah's headmaster. "You must observe everything carefully."

"You'll have to be a little mother to Gavin now," Joey's mum clucked at her.

Norah was told to dress warmly, not to pick up Canadian slang and to remember she was English. And again and again she heard the words, "Take care of Gavin."

Gavin told everyone that Creature was excited about going on a train and a ship. That was as much as he seemed to grasp. "They're sending us away!" Norah wanted to shout. But there was no point in upsetting him.

Grandad glowered at the visitors from a corner of the kitchen, where he sat with his pipe and newspaper. He was allowed to sulk; Norah had to be polite and submit to all the kissing, patting and advice.

Not all the neighbours approved. "I couldn't send my children so far away," whispered Mrs Baker to Mrs Maybourne. "What about German torpedoes — have they considered that?"

"Shhhh!" her husband warned, with a glance at Norah, who was getting used to pretending she didn't hear things.

Why couldn't Mrs Baker tell that to Mum and Dad? But Grandad had mentioned it too, and Dad said that staying in England was a greater risk than U-boats.

In church the next day the Smith girls waved at Norah importantly, as if their shared fate made them allies.

"The last hymn is for our five young travellers who are about to start on a great adventure," announced Reverend Smith. "Number 301". His eyes glistened as he gazed at his three children in the front pew.

"O hear us when we cry to thee / For those in peril on the sea," droned the congregation.

"How could he!" hissed Norah's mother. She refused to sing and glared at the vicar, whom she had never liked.

Norah could sense the whole churchful of sympathetic eyes fastened on her back. She gripped her hymn book and sang without thinking of the words.

After church, more people milled around the door to say goodbye. Dulcie and Lucy, dressed alike as usual, skipped over. Dulcie, who often acted afraid of Norah, was unusually forward. "Oh, Norah, isn't it exciting! I'm so glad we're going where it's safe. I wish Mummy and Daddy could come too, but they have to stay and help win the war."

"*We* should be staying to help win the war," said Norah coldly.

"But we're not old enough! Daddy says children are better out of the way."

"Not old enough": that's what Norah's sisters had said to her all her life. Even after Gavin had arrived, she had had to spend a lot of time proving she was old enough. She scowled at Dulcie, who had always reminded her of a calf, with her mild, bulging eyes and dull expression. Just because they were stuck together on this journey, it would never do to let Dulcie think they were going to be friends.

"Are you bringing all your dolls with you, Goosey?" Norah taunted.

Dulcie wilted at the familiar nickname, the way she did at school. Norah felt as guilty as she always did when she teased her. The guilt made her even more irritated.

"Thank you, we would appreciate a ride into town," Mum was saying to Mrs Smith. "Are you sure you can spare the petrol? Come along, Norah, we still have a lot of packing to do."

Everyone at church had commented on the unusually calm sky. But the air-raid siren sounded right in the middle of Sunday dinner. Dad rushed off and Mum made them all go into the shelter in the garden.

"Can't I watch?" begged Norah. "It might be the last fight I see."

"Not after that German plane," said Mum grimly.

Norah and Grandad peeked out of the low entrance of the corrugated steel structure while Mum read to Gavin on one of the narrow bunks. Grandad had hardly spoken since Saturday morning, but he squeezed Norah's shoulder as they watched the planes soar over.

There was fighting on and off for the rest of the day. Norah was made to stay either inside the shelter or in the house, helping to pack. They were only allowed to take one piece of luggage each.

"I can't fit in any more," sighed Mum that night. She sat on the end of Norah's bed, folding the last of the freshly washed and ironed clothes into the small brown suitcase. "I hope I've packed enough woollies. We'll send more clothes to you later."

She glanced around Norah's room. It had belonged to Muriel and Tibby, but Norah had claimed it after they left. Three neglected dolls sat demurely under the window. The ceiling was hung with balsa-wood aeroplanes, twisting slightly in the warm night air. Mum looked back at Norah, already in bed and escaping into a *Hotspur* comic.

"Is there anything else you want to take? One of your planes, perhaps?"

"No thank you," said Norah stiffly. She had already packed her shrapnel and a few comics. Mum was in disguise again, as bright and cheerful as if this weren't Norah's last night at home.

"I wish I knew more about Canada to tell you. I imagine it will be beautiful, though — like *Anne of Green Gables*. And the Dionne Quintuplets live in Canada. Just imagine, five little girls exactly alike! Perhaps you'll see them!"

She looked desperate when Norah didn't answer. "Wait . . . " Mum left the room and returned in a few seconds with the family photograph that always stood on the mantelpiece. "I want you to have this, Norah. I'll wrap it in your blue jersey."

Norah just grunted. Mum sat down again, patted her hand and sighed. "I know you're angry with us. I don't blame you, but wait until you get on the ship and start having a good time! It won't be as bad as you think, I promise. I wish I knew who will be taking care of you, but Dad's right — they're sure to be kind. Just don't judge them too soon. You know how stubborn you can be." She smiled. "And try not to lose your temper. You've inherited that from me, I'm afraid. But you've always been so sure of yourself, I'm not really worried about you, Norah. *You're* tough, but Gavin isn't. He's so sensitive, and he's very young to be going so far away. You'll have to take especially good care of him." Her voice broke.

Norah yawned deliberately. "I'm going to sleep now." She flopped over and buried her face in her pillow. What about *her*? She, too, was young to be going so far away, wasn't she? Gavin had always been Mum's favourite, though, just as Norah was Dad's.

Mum kissed the back of Norah's neck. "Goodnight, sweetheart. Go right to sleep — you have a big day tomorrow."

The Smiths were supposed to pick them up after dinner. Norah spent the morning hanging about outside the house. She looked for the hedgehog they left bowls of milk for, but he had disappeared — perhaps the air-raid sirens had frightened him away. She filled the stirrup-pump with water from the red fire bucket by the back door and sprinkled the carrots with it. Finally she sat glumly on the step and watched the silly chickens scratching in the dirt.

Mum made her and Gavin have a bath before dinner. She washed their hair, cut their nails and dressed them in clean clothes from the skin out. Dad had polished their shoes until they were as glossy as chestnuts. When he arrived home for dinner, they sat down to an extra-special meal. But Norah could only push her fishcakes around her plate.

"The Smiths' car is going to be awfully crowded," said Dad. "Why don't you cycle into town with me, Norah? If we leave now, we'll have plenty of time before the train."

"Oh, yes, please!" she said. In the holidays she often went into Gilden with her father.

"But you'll get your dress dirty," protested her mother. "I want you to look nice. You know how tidy Dulcie and Lucy always are."

"She'll get grubby on the train anyhow," said Dad. "Say goodbye to Grandad and we'll leave now."

But Grandad was nowhere to be found. "We already said goodbye," mumbled Norah. Last night he had hugged her fiercely and pressed a sixpence into her hand. "You keep fighting, young one," he whispered. Norah couldn't answer. It seemed so unfair that Grandad had come to live with them just as she had to leave.

She and Dad rode down the main street side by side. Norah tried to fix the familiar landmarks in her mind. The village pond, where she and Tom fished for tench. The wide green that was now littered with old bedsprings, hayricks and kitchen ranges to stop enemy planes from landing. Tom's mother's shop, where she spent most of her pocket money on sweets and comics.

As they reached the edge of the village and Mrs Chandler's house, she kept her head down in case the Skywatchers were in the Lookout, watching her go by. She hadn't seen them again; there were enough goodbyes to say as it was.

They rode through the peaceful countryside in silence. The early afternoon sky was overcast and grey. "Maybe it will rain at last," said Dad. "There won't be any fighting today." Norah looked up automatically, but there was only a flock of black and white lapwings overhead, veering like Spitfires and crying plaintively.

"Let's rest here a minute." Dad pulled over to the stile leading to Stumble Wood. Norah leaned her bicycle against it and Dad lifted her up to sit on top. A cloud of white butterflies hovered in the cool air.

"How will you get my bicycle back to Ringden?" she asked, gazing sadly at its worn leather seat. It was old, black and ugly, a hand-me-down from Tibby, but it was her favourite possession.

"Someone from work can ride it back. Don't worry, I'll keep it shipshape for your return. Now, Norah . . . "

Norah tried to avoid his eyes; not *another* pep talk.

"I want you to remember three things," said Dad gravely. "Most important, of course, is to take care of Gavin. I don't think he really knows he's going away from us and perhaps that's for the best. But when he realizes, he may become very upset — you'll have to comfort him. The second is that you aren't just going to Canada as yourself. You're representing England. If you're impolite or ungrateful, the Canadians will think that's what English children are like. So remember your manners and whenever you're in doubt, think of how Mum and I would expect you to behave. And third . . . " He finally smiled, "Have a good time! I know you will. Just think, you're the first one in the family to go overseas! I wish I'd had the opportunity to travel more when I was young."

He really was envious, Norah realized, not just jollying her along. Dad had worked for most of his life as a bookkeeper in the tannery in Gilden; the only time he'd been away was in the first war.

Norah swallowed hard. "Oh, Dad . . . do I *have* to go?"

Dad looked sympathetic, but said softly, "Yes, Norah — you have to go. I'm sorry, but you just have to believe me when I tell you it's for the best. Come along now, we'd better carry on."

They reached the Gilden railway station just as the Smiths' blue car drew up. Dulcie and Lucy jumped out, wearing smocked pink dresses and pink straw hats. Derek was in his grammar school uniform. Gavin rushed over to the engine.

"I wish I could come to London with you," said Dad. He pulled Gavin back from the tracks and picked him up. "Goodbye, old man. You do exactly what Norah says."

"Say goodbye to Creature," ordered Gavin. Dad shook the elephant's trunk solemnly.

He handed Norah a twisted white bag. "Sweets for the train," he winked. "Now remember what I told you. And have a safe and happy journey, my brave Norah." He kissed her quickly and turned his head, but Norah had seen his tears.

She stomped after her mother onto the train. If Dad was so upset, then why was he doing this to her? She glared at the Smiths in the opposite seat, chattering to their father, who was able to spare the time to come to London.

Steam drifted by the window and Norah could hardly make out her father's waving arm. When the mist cleared, she waved back and forced herself to smile.

For the next two hours, Norah almost forgot why they were going to London. The only other time she had been was the Christmas before last, when Muriel and Tibby had taken her to see *Peter Pan*. This journey seemed the same. The train still chuffed along sounding important, they still waited until after Ashford to eat their sandwiches and she couldn't shake off the familiar train feeling of having a treat.

But there were differences too: the large number of men and women in uniform, the whited-out station signs they passed and the fine netting on the windows in case of flying glass. There was only a small hole left in the middle to peek through.

And this time she didn't even see London. They went straight from one train station to another via the underground. Dozens of other children and parents waited for the train north. The children were all, like Norah, carrying luggage and coats and gas mask cases, and they all had large labels attached to them, as if they were going to be sent through the post. Some of the younger ones, like Gavin and Lucy, also clutched stuffed animals or dolls. Most of the crowd babbled in high, excited voices; others were quiet and wary. "Is Your Journey Really Necessary?" asked a poster on the wall.

Norah was introduced to a fat, flustered woman called Miss Nott. "I'm your train escort," she explained. She consulted a list. "Is this all the Kent and Sussex children? Say goodbye, then — we must go on board."

The train waited, a snorting black dragon. Norah gulped and took her mother's hand.

"Oh, Norah . . . " Mum smoothed Norah's hair, refastened it at the side, and pulled down her felt hat. "Hang onto your coats carefully," she said. "Remember that your five pounds and your papers are sewn inside." She kissed Norah's forehead. "Make sure you both clean your teeth every night." All she said to Gavin was a choked "Goodbye, pet — you take care of Creature." Then she helped him on with his rucksack and put his hand in Norah's.

"Come on," muttered Norah, pulling Gavin's arm as Miss Nott beckoned.

"Are we going on the other train now?" asked Gavin with delight. They were whisked into the compartment with the rest of their group and couldn't get close enough to the window to wave goodbye.

VI

"Are We Downhearted?"

The eight children under the charge of Miss Nott were crammed into one compartment. Derek was the eldest and Gavin the youngest. Two of the children across from Norah were boys around Lucy's age. They had brought along cards, and Lucy and Gavin joined their game of snap on the floor. The other stranger was a cheerful older girl called Margery. She tried to talk to them, but Dulcie was too shy to answer and Norah didn't feel like being friendly.

She read all her comics, and then there was nothing to do. She couldn't even look out the window, which had been closed and blacked out for the evening. "Do you know where we're going?" she asked Derek. He was also being unsociable, his face hidden behind his book.

Derek looked insulted at being spoken to by someone his sister's age. "Liverpool, I imagine," he said shortly, in the posh accent he'd picked up at his school.

They all ate their sandwiches, and the compartment became a smelly mess of greasy papers, crumbs and spilt milk. Miss Nott and Margery darted around trying to tidy up. Then Miss Nott's plump figure swayed in the corridor while she led a singalong : "Run Rabbit Run", "Roll Out the Barrel" and "There'll Always Be an England". Dulcie joined in dutifully, but Norah refused.

The singing began to falter as the children grew drowsy. Gavin fell asleep and Norah tried to pull her cramped arm from under him. Finally she dozed off herself, the train's chant intruding into her dreams: Don't *want* to go, don't *want* to go, don't *want* to go . . .

They arrived in Liverpool early in the morning. Miss Nott said goodbye, looking relieved to be free of them. The dazed and hungry children were driven to a hostel at the edge of the city where they spent the next few days, eating at long tables and sleeping in long rows on straw pallets on the floor. The hostel filled up with children from all over Britain, many with strong accents that were hard to decipher. Norah began to feel like a performing puppet. Again and again she was asked to follow someone, to get ready for bed, to get up, to eat, to play games and to sing rousing songs.

On the first day a doctor examined her and pronounced her "scrawny but fit". The next morning an earnest and important-looking man told the assembled children, as Dad had, that they were little ambassadors. "When things go wrong, as they often will, remember you are British and grin and bear it. Be truthful, brave, kind and grateful."

Norah stored this advice at the back of her mind along with all the other she had received and promptly forgot it. The only person's she followed was Mum's: she carefully cleaned her teeth every evening. It was somehow soothing to do such a simple task.

As for looking after Gavin, she left that up to the women in charge. She waved to him in the morning and reminded him to clean *his* teeth at night. But she had too much to brood about to consider him in between. Besides, he wasn't making a fuss, although he looked bewildered and whispered a lot to Creature.

On the third morning they were taken on a bus to the wharves. It took most of the day to board the ship. First they were herded into a cavernous shed called the Embarkation Area. Hundreds of children raced about while harried-looking escorts tried to find their groups.

Norah's escort was Miss Montague-Scott. She was an enthusiastic, strong woman with springy brown curls, much livelier than the frazzled Miss Nott. Norah had already met her at the hostel; Miss Montague-Scott would take care of them all the way to Canada. There were fifteen children in her group, including Dulcie and Lucy, all of them girls. But now Miss Montague-Scott was leading Gavin up to them.

"Here she is! Norah, we've decided Gavin's too young to go with the boys. He'll stay with us and sleep in your cabin."

Norah looked over her brother doubtfully; now she'd *have* to look after him. She'd never had to before;

Mum or Muriel or Tibby always had.

Gavin's cheeks were as flushed as if he had a fever. "Are we going on the ship now, Norah? Will Muv and Dad be on the ship too?"

Oh *no*! Didn't he realize? Norah looked around frantically for Miss Montague-Scott, but she had hurried away to organize someone else.

She couldn't tell him — then he'd cry and everyone would expect her to do something. "Hold on to me, we're supposed to follow the others," she muttered, ignoring his question.

A woman fastened a small hard disc stamped with a number around Norah's neck. Another official checked their identity cards and passports and made sure they didn't have too much luggage. Then someone collected all their gas masks. "You won't need these any more," she smiled.

Norah clutched hers possessively. "Can't I keep it as a souvenir?"

"You have enough to carry," said the woman. Norah handed over the cardboard case she'd taken with her everywhere for the past year. She was surprised to discover she felt attached to it; she'd always hated wearing her gas mask for school drills. It smelled like hot rubber and made her want to gag. But you could produce rude noises and spit by puffing into it, and once she'd sent her whole class into convulsions by pretending to blow its long "nose". Without it she felt naked and vulnerable.

Miss Montague-Scott led her group to the wharf. They sat down and waited for hours to board the SS

Zandvoort. Sandwiches were passed down the long lines of children, and then a man started them singing. Were they going to have to sing all the way to Canada?

"Come along, everyone," the man exhorted through his megaphone. "Stand up and take some d-e-e-e-e-p breaths. Now, all together . . . 'There'll *al*-ways *be* an *Eng*-land . . .'"

It sounded like a dirge. A group of boys behind them broke into the singing loudly: "There'll always be a SCOTLAND . . . " Norah turned around and grinned with surprise.

The leader looked startled, then he smiled too. "Good for you, boys, that's the spirit! Now, kiddies, you're about to start on a marvellous adventure. I see some sad faces in the crowd — that will never do. Are we downhearted?"

A few voices called out "No!"

"I can't hear you! *Everyone*, now — are we downhearted?"

"NO!" roared the children.

Dulcie was standing beside Norah; her hysterical scream pierced Norah's right ear. Again and again the man led the crowd to yell "NO!"

Norah pressed her lips tightly together. This was as bad as being asked to clap if you believed in fairies.

"That's much better!" laughed the jolly leader. "Now, before you sit down again — thumbs up! Come on, everyone, show me how!"

"Thumbs up, Norah!" said Dulcie, closing her fists and pointing her thumbs. She looked puzzled when Norah ignored her.

Finally they were allowed to walk up the gangway to the huge, grey ship. Norah sniffed in a mixture of tar, steam and salt water. In spite of herself, she felt a twinge of excitement. She'd never been on a ship before.

"Smile, everyone!" They were asked to lean over the railing, wave to the photographers and drone once again, "There'll Always Be an England".

Norah held onto Gavin's small hot palm and took a last look at Britain. Everything was grey: the dirty water below, the smoking chimneys of Liverpool and the leaden sky. Slender beams of searchlights crisscrossed the dusk and high in the air floated the silvery, pig-shaped barrage balloons.

Then the engines thrummed, the whistles blew and the ship began to move. Norah turned her back on home and faced the other way.

VII

The Voyage

Norah and Gavin were assigned to the same cabin as Goosey and Loosey. "Isn't this nice for you!" boomed Miss Montague-Scott, popping her head in to tell them to get ready for bed. "Four friends from home bunking together!"

It was awful. Dulcie giggled as they banged into each other in the cramped space. Lucy complained because her nightdress was wrinkled. Worst of all was Gavin. He looked around the cabin frantically, then shook Norah's arm. "Where are Muv and Dad? Why haven't they come yet?"

Norah wanted to shake him. How could he be so dim? "They aren't *here*," she said impatiently. "Don't be so silly. They're at home in Ringden and we're going to Canada without them."

"Didn't you know that, Gavin?" said Lucy with all the superiority of someone seven years old. "We aren't going to see our mothers and fathers for a long, *long* time, not until the war is over."

"Of course he knows," snapped Norah. "Clean your teeth, Gavin." She tried to find their toothbrushes in the clutter.

But Gavin just sat on his bunk looking stunned. He fingered his elephant. "Creature said they would be on the ship," he whispered.

"Well, they aren't." He continued to sit passively, so Norah undressed him, put on his pyjamas and tried to tuck him into his bed.

"I want to sleep with you," said Gavin in a small voice.

Norah tried to control her irritation. "Oh, all right." It was difficult to find enough room for both of them in the narrow space, but finally they slept.

Norah woke up with a start a few hours later. Where was she? Her bed was vibrating and there was a low, humming sound. Then she remembered and moved her leg from under Gavin's. She brushed across a cold, wet patch.

"Gavin!" Norah sat up and shook him angrily. "Look what you've done!" She made him get up and stand shivering on the cabin floor while she stripped the sheets and covered the damp mattress with blankets.

"Gavin wet the be-ed, Gavin wet the be-ed," crowed Lucy in the morning. "He's a *baby.*"

He did it every night. Because he insisted on sleeping with Norah, she made him curl up at the other end of the bed, but she still woke up every morning to the wetness. Miss Montague-Scott helped her rinse out the sheet and his pyjama bottoms every morning in the tiny sink, but they never dried properly and she could never get it all out. Soon there was a perpetual sharp odour in the cabin, and Norah spent as much time as she could away from it.

Gavin followed her around like a lost puppy. After Norah had pulled his grey balaclava helmet over his head on the first windy day, he refused to take it off. He wore it to meals and even to bed. It made his round blue eyes look even larger and more frightened. He had become strangely silent and didn't even talk to Creature. Norah knew she should soothe him, but what could she say? She couldn't tell him they'd see their parents soon — they wouldn't. She couldn't think of anything comforting about Canada to offer him. And she couldn't help nagging him to stop being so babyish.

Then she got a reprieve. On the third day at sea, she and Gavin sneaked up to the upper-class decks. The government-sponsored children were supposed to stay below, but no one noticed if they didn't. Many of the children above were under five and several had mothers, nannies and other adults travelling with them. Norah found a place to sit beside a friendly looking mother with a baby in a carry-cot beside her.

"Hello, you two." She smiled at Gavin. "Aren't you hot in that hat?"

Gavin shook his head, but he took out Creature for the first time since they'd boarded and held him up to the woman.

"What a very nice elephant. What do you call him?"

"Creature," whispered Gavin.

The woman laughed. "That's an unusual name. Where does it come from?"

Norah explained how Gavin had named the elephant after the line in the Sunday school hymn: "All Creatures Great and Small."

"He's very small for an elephant, you see," said Gavin. "What's *your* name?"

"Mrs Pym. And this is my little boy, Timothy. We're going to Montreal to live with Timothy's grandparents."

After that, Gavin spent all his time trailing after Mrs Pym. She didn't seem to mind; she even took him into meals with her and came down to kiss him goodnight every evening. Norah felt vaguely guilty about abandoning him, but he seemed much happier with Mrs Pym than he was with her.

Now that she was free of Gavin, she longed to spend the whole of each day exploring the ship. But Miss Montague-Scott had other ideas. You could tell she was a teacher; she seemed to forget that it was still the holidays. Some of the other escorts were lax and spent a lot of their time in the lounge or flirting with the officers, but Miss Montague-Scott made her group conform to the ship's schedule. First there were prayers, then a lifeboat drill, then a different activity each day: singalongs on the poop deck, art classes, spelling bees, Physical Training or memorizing poems. "No grumpy faces allowed in *my* group, Norah," she cried heartily as they performed their morning jack-knives. "*One*, two, *one*, two . . . "

Then Miss Montague-Scott got seasick. So did Lucy and many other children. Some threw up on the deck as they ran around, but most spent their days moaning in bed.

Now Norah was free to do as she pleased. Dulcie wasn't seasick either, and when she wasn't looking after Lucy, she hung around with Margery and some other prissy girls who had formed a society called the "Thumbs Up Club".

"Don't you want to join us, Norah?" Dulcie asked. "It keeps our spirits up. Every time one of us feels homesick or scared she says 'thumbs up!' and we all do it together. It's a great help."

"*I'm* not homesick," lied Norah, who lay beside Gavin every night trying to block out the images of home that flooded her mind. "I'm busy with much more important things, thank you."

She was watching for periscopes. Every day she leaned over the railing and gazed out to sea. Ahead of the SS *Zandvoort* steamed a whole convoy of ships, protecting them until they were far enough away from England to be safe. The escorts pretended to ignore the presence of the convoy, but Norah remembered Mrs Baker's comment. *She* knew they were in danger of being torpedoed. She watched the unbroken line of grey water on the horizon every day for an hour, until she got too chilled to stand still. The problem was, she didn't know what a periscope or a U-boat looked like.

Sometimes, if she let herself think too much about torpedoes, the suffocating fear would come again.

Once she groped beside her in panic — where was her gas mask? Then she remembered. Instead of a gas mask, she now had a lifebelt she had to carry everywhere: scratchy orange canvas filled with cork. At least it made a good pillow.

The ship was like a moving island and Norah explored every inch of it, happy to be able to go where she wanted after the regimented hostel. The Dutch crew indulged the children and let them help polish brass and coil ropes. Sometimes the captain would stop and speak to them in his halting English, or inspect their lifeboat drill. Wherever he went, he was followed by a gang of admiring small boys.

The best part of the voyage was the unrationed food. Everyone gorged on unlimited supplies of sugar, butter, oranges and ice cream. Some of the meals had seven courses and there were five a day. Norah thought of the doctor who'd said she was scrawny, and ate as much as she could.

The ten-day trip became a soothing, timeless space between the war behind and the unknown country ahead. Everything had happened so fast that Norah still couldn't believe she was leaving home. Sometimes she tried to imagine "Canada". She thought of ice and snow, red-coated Mounties and *Anne of Green Gables*. None of it fit together.

Miss Montague-Scott recovered but, except for the daily lifeboat drills, she gave up trying to organize them. "They may as well run free while they can," Norah heard her tell another escort. "The poor kiddies are going to have enough red tape when they arrive."

What was red tape? Norah wondered.

She made friends with one of the boys from the Scottish group. His name was Jamie, and he had collected far more shrapnel than she had. He helped her watch for periscopes "I *do* wish we'd be torpedoed," Jamie said longingly, as they stared at the blank expanse of water. When they got tired of keeping watch they held up biscuits for the hovering gulls to snatch out of their fingers.

Jamie introduced Norah to his older brothers. She envied them when they told her they were going to live with their uncle on the Canadian prairies. The Smiths, too, were "nominated". That meant they knew whom they were going to stay with in Ontario. "It will be in a vicarage in Toronto, just like at home," said Dulcie. "The Milnes are old friends of Daddy's." Norah wondered where she and Gavin would be sleeping in a week.

Norah and Jamie were standing together on the deck one morning when Norah cried, "Look! Is that land?"

Far in the distance was a thin blue line, as if someone had painted a dark outline along the horizon. As the day progressed it got darker and closer, and the next morning it had broken up into islands.

Then a thick fog obscured their vision. Jamie's brother, Alistair, who seemed to know everything, told them they were off the Grand Banks of Newfoundland. As they leaned over the railing into the mist, Norah was astonished to see an enormous grey-white shape loom out of the fog.

"What's *that*?"

"It's an iceberg!" said Alistair. "There's something to write home about!" They watched in awe as the ship glided by the ghostly mountain of ice.

Soon they entered a huge estuary; Alistair said it was the St Lawrence River but its banks were so far apart it seemed more like a small sea. Then it narrowed to a proper river, its high shore dense with firs. Jamie kept a close watch. "Maybe we'll spot an Indian war dance," he told Norah.

"What a little idiot!" scoffed Alistair. "Canada isn't like a wild west film."

But Jamie and Norah kept examining the cliffs hopefully. Now they were passing small villages, each with a lighthouse and a white-spired church. In the distance rose the green roofs of Quebec City. The ship docked there briefly and all the children crowded at the railing, pushing each other in their excitement. Below them men shouted to each other in French.

"Don't they speak English in Canada?" Norah asked Margery nervously. What would it be like to live with a new family she didn't understand?

Margery looked bewildered but Miss Montague-Scott assured them that, although Canada had two languages, most of the people in Ontario spoke English. "The children who will be living in Montreal are lucky," she added in her school-teacher tone. "Some of them will probably learn French." But Norah thought it was going to be difficult enough to adjust in her own language.

The ship continued through the dusk to Montreal. That evening there was an excited atmosphere aboard.

They had a special banquet, and the escorts led the children in a chorus of "For they are jolly good fellows." The captain stood up and told them what good sailors they'd been.

They were allowed to open the darkened portholes for the first time, and all the ship's lights streamed out into the darkness. "You're safe now," laughed Miss Montague-Scott. "There's no need for a black-out any more." She had come in to help their cabin pack. "Make sure you have all your papers ready. We'll be in Montreal in an hour and will stay there for the night. Then I'll have to leave you — someone else will be in charge."

"Where will you go?" asked Norah. Miss Montague-Scott already seemed to be an established part of their lives.

"Back to Britain and, I hope, back here again with another load of evacuees," she said cheerfully. "Let's hope I can conquer my seasickness next time! Now, Gavin, can't you take off that dreadful hat? You'll get some kind of skin disease, you've worn it so long." She pulled at his balaclava.

"No!" wailed Gavin, pressing his hands to his head.

Miss Montague-Scott sighed. "You'll have to find a way to get it off him, Norah. It's not healthy."

Norah didn't have time to worry about it. It was hard enough getting Gavin to leave Mrs Pym the next morning. She gripped his hand tightly when he started to run after her. "I'm your *sister!*" she hissed. "She's not even related to you. You have to stay with me, so do what I say."

The timeless peace of the voyage was over; now everything was confusing and difficult again, the way it had been in Liverpool. Baggage was piled everywhere. All morning they lined up on board the hot ship, until their landing cards were checked and their passports stamped. Then they waited again, in the observation room, where at least they could sit down. Some journalists came on board to take their pictures.

"Isn't this exciting, Norah?" said Dulcie. "It's as if we were famous!" Her voice had an hysterical edge to it and there was an ugly rash all around her mouth from constantly licking her lips. A reporter came up to them and Dulcie began telling him about the "Thumbs Up Club."

Finally they were allowed to walk down a covered gangway. A large crowd clapped and cheered, throwing them sweets and chewing gum. Then their papers were checked again by customs officers with soft accents. "What a brave little girl, to travel all the way from England by yourself!" said the man helping Norah. He spoke as if she were Gavin's age.

"Over here, Norah!" called Dulcie. Norah frowned. Dulcie was getting much too bossy.

The Ontario group was moved towards a bus that was to go to the Montreal train station. Norah peered through the noisy crowd for Jamie and spotted him in another line, too far away to call to. But she'd never see him again, anyway; what was the use in saying goodbye?

Mrs Pym hurried up and gave Gavin a last kiss. "You do what your big sister says," she told him.

"Cheerio, Norah, and the best of luck to both of you."
She looked as if she felt sorry for them; Norah thrust
out her hand quickly so Mrs Pym wouldn't kiss her as
well.

She dragged her brother onto the bus before he
had time to whimper. The bus pulled away from both
Mrs Pym and Jamie, leaving Norah and Gavin alone
with each other once again.

The Montreal train station was a vast, clean hall
with a slippery marble floor; the enormous space
echoed with voices. Margery pointed to the ceiling.
"There's the Canadian flag," she said knowingly. Norah
gazed at the tiny Union Jack lost in a sea of red. It was
like England now — small and far away.

The train to Toronto was different from British
trains: there were no compartments and all the seats
faced the same way. Norah and Gavin sat across the
aisle from a stout man with a checked hat. He seemed
very curious about them.

"All the way from England, eh? How old are you?
Did you get bombed yet? Where's your village?"

He asked so many questions that Norah won-
dered if he were a spy. "I can't say," she said loudly, the
way their headmaster had told them to answer suspicious strangers. She stared so hard at him that he got
up and moved to another seat.

Seventy children from the ship were going to
Toronto. There were new women in charge and one of
them went up and down the carriage, passing out
coloured armbands. Norah's was blue and Gavin's

green. She supposed they signified their ages.

"Will we be staying with our new families tonight?" Norah asked her.

"Oh, no, dear. You'll be put into residences at the university for a while, until we get you vetted."

"Vetted?"

The woman laughed. "Just checking you over to make sure you're healthy. Then your hosts will come and pick you up. Don't worry, we have lots of fun planned. Singalongs and games and movies and swimming."

Norah sighed . . . *more* singing.

"My sisters and I won't have to go there, will we? asked Derek behind her. "We know who we're living with."

"That's nice, dear, but you still have to stay at the university at first. Regulations, I'm afraid."

Norah was glad; the Smiths needed to be taken down a peg.

Gavin had fallen asleep. He twitched awake when the train drew to a stop. It was already dusk — where had this blurry day gone? Many of the children had dozed and someone had pulled down the blinds to keep out the rays of the setting sun.

Now one of the adults pushed up the blind beside them. "There you are! Welcome to Toronto!"

Lights blazed outside the window, some in beautiful flashing colours. Norah gaped, amazed.

Gavin took one look and screamed. "Turn out the lights, turn out the lights!"

"It's all *right*, Gavin!" Norah pushed him back into

his seat. "Remember what Miss Montague-Scott said? There's no black-out here. There's no war. We're in Canada, now, not England."

She choked on the last words. Now what would happen? Gathering up their things wearily, she got up to leave the train.

VIII

Guests of War

At Union Station another set of adults conducted them off the train and asked them to line up two by two. They were led into a large waiting room where a man gave orders.

"Welcome to Toronto, children!" He made the name sound like "Trawna". "We want each of you to look at the colour of your armband and line up behind the leader with that colour."

He didn't need to shout; the whole group was tired and subdued. Norah looked around for the adult wearing a blue armband. Then she remembered that Gavin had a different colour. Her brother clung to her dress, his grimy face spotted with tear marks.

"Please . . . " she entreated an adult. "My little brother's supposed to go with the green group, but he has to stay with me."

The woman looked worried. "Oh, but he's supposed to go with the boys. You can visit him later." She gently loosened Gavin's fingers and led him away. He looked back over his shoulder at Norah, his eyes brimming.

"I'll see you later, Gavin!" called Norah. If only Mrs Pym were still here.

"He'll be all right, Norah," said Dulcie. Norah felt almost envious of her. She never seemed to have any problems with Lucy, but Lucy was far more confident than her big sister. And they both had Derek to look after them, even if he was usually lost behind a book.

That morning Dulcie had dressed Lucy and herself in their pink dresses, which she'd hung up and kept clean for the whole journey. Norah's dress was stained with food and her feet were moist and gritty inside her socks.

"Come along, Blues." The group of girls followed their leader out of the station to a waiting bus decorated with a blue pennant.

Just as in Montreal, a crowd across the street began to applaud. They strained against a rope as they called out greetings. "Welcome to Canada!" "Rule Britannia!" "Look at them, aren't they sweet?" As the blue group came closer, a sigh rose in the crowd. A woman near Norah said, "Do you see those two? The ones in matching pink dresses and hats? They look just like the Princesses!" Lucy smiled and waved as if they were.

The bus ride was short and soon they were unloaded at an old stone building the adults called Hart House. It was like a church inside, with dark ceiling beams and high windows of coloured glass.

Gavin rushed up from a group of boys. "You went away," he sniffed. His nose was running disgustingly. Norah tried to mop it with the corner of her dress; she had lost her handkerchief long ago.

A jovial man led Gavin back to his group. "Come along, youngster, you're eating with the big fellows!" Norah lost sight of him as they were taken into a vast dining room called the Great Hall. It had large golden letters painted around its walls.

Supper was boiled chicken and mushy cauli-flower. By the time dessert arrived, some of the children had begun to revive. They called to one another down the long tables and bolted their ice cream. But Norah wasn't hungry.

Immediately after supper the girls were taken into a gymnasium where they had to stand in their vests and knickers while women doctors checked their throats, ears and chests. "We need to put some flesh on you," the doctor told Norah. She felt insulted — hadn't she eaten a lot on the ship? She'd always been small for her age, but no one had ever made a fuss about it before.

While she got dressed again, she heard the doctor tell the little girl behind her that she had a cold and would have to go straight to the infirmary. "But I want to stay with my sister," the child wailed.

A nurse opened the door and hurried across the room. "Is Norah Stoakes here?"

Norah waved her arm. "Can you come and stop your brother from crying?" the nurse asked her. "He's having hysterics because we took off his hat, poor little tyke."

Gavin's screams filled the corridor. He was outside the other gymnasium, thrashing and kicking on the floor. "I want my s-sister!" he blubbered.

Norah wasn't at all sure she wanted *him*. His cheeks were smeared with dirt and mucus and his fair hair looked dark where the balaclava had covered it. What would Mum do? She was suddenly furious that her mother wasn't there to cope.

"Shut *up*, Gavin!" She shook him so hard that his head wobbled.

The nurse looked shocked and reached out to stop her. "Don't be so rough, Norah! That's no way to treat your little brother!"

As Gavin's cries turned into hiccups, Norah whirled around and faced the woman. "You *asked* me to stop him, and I did! It's your fault he was crying, anyway — you shouldn't have taken his hat off! Didn't you realize that would upset him?"

The nurse looked indignant. "We had to take it off — it was filthy! We've thrown it away and now he'll have to have his hair washed thoroughly. You look as if you could do with a bath too, Miss — come with me. And I think you're forgetting your manners. In Canada, children don't speak like that to their elders."

She led them outside and across the grass to another building, where there was a row of bathtubs. Norah lay dazed in the soothing hot water, listening to Gavin having his hair shampooed in the next cubicle. He had turned silent again.

"Do I have to bathe you as well?" grumbled the nurse, coming in to check on her. "Imagine, a girl of your age who can't wash herself!" She did Norah's hair and scrubbed her all over with a rough flannel. Then she handed her a kind of gown to put on.

"Now say good-night to your brother," she ordered. "I'll take him to his room and come back for you. Yours is in a different building."

A stubborn voice forced itself up through Norah's exhaustion. "No."

"What did you say?"

"He has to stay with me."

"Don't be difficult, Norah. You can see him all you want during the day, but the boys and the girls are sleeping in separate residences."

"No," said Norah again. Part of her wondered why she was being so insistent; she didn't really want the care of Gavin. But he looked so pathetic with his wet hair skinned back and dark circles under his eyes. She tried to forget about how her hands had made his thin neck bend like the stem of a flower.

The nurse stared at her for a few seconds, then gave up. "Stay here," she sighed. "I'll see what I can do. But you're upsetting our system."

In ten minutes Norah got her way. The nurse returned and took them both to a building called Falconer House, to a room with four beds in it. Norah's luggage was already there and a boy arrived with Gavin's just as they did. The beds were labelled and Norah noticed that the others belonged to Goosey and Loosey.

"I have to go, but someone will check on you in a few minutes," said the nurse. Her voice was kinder now, but Norah was too tired to answer her.

"Get into bed," she told Gavin after the nurse had left. He obeyed mutely, curling into a tight ball. Norah tucked the blanket around him. She felt the mattress and was relieved to find a rubber sheet.

She buried herself in her own stiff, clean sheets. She was so worn out, she scarcely heard the Smiths when they came in a few minutes later.

They stayed at the university for a week. Everyone was very kind and welcoming, but Norah began to feel she was in prison. The campus grounds were spacious and she longed to run on her own under the large trees or cross the busy street, where the cars drove on the wrong side. The bustling city surrounding the university seemed as big and exciting as London. But Boy Scouts stood on guard all day outside Hart House, where the children ate and played. "They're to keep away curious strangers," the adults said, but Norah thought they were to keep them in.

The only time the children left the campus was for a visit to a hospital, where each of them was examined in much more detail than in either Hart House or Liverpool. Norah had to take off all her clothes while a doctor checked every inch of her body, from her hair to her toes, including the embarrassing parts in the middle. She was X-rayed, her knees were hammered and a blood sample was taken from her finger. Then she was given several injections and pushed and prodded until her body didn't seem to belong to her any more. Canadians seemed to think that British children carried some dreadful disease.

Another doctor asked her questions: what her parents were like, who her friends were at home, and what she liked to do best. It was so painful to talk about home that Norah answered him in short, clipped sentences. When he asked her in his kind voice how she felt about being evacuated, she just mumbled "Fine" to keep from crying. "I guess you're a shy one," said the doctor. "You'll soon feel more talkative in your new family."

Once more, Gavin was taken off her hands. Now he trailed after Miss Carmichael, who looked after their dormitory and, as well, was in charge of all the children under nine. She was a softer, prettier version of Miss Montague-Scott; not as hearty, but just as schoolteacherish.

"What a well-behaved child Gavin is!" said Miss Carmichael. "And such an attractive little boy, with those huge eyes and delicate features." She kept the younger children constantly occupied. Gavin came back to the room each evening with paint on his clothes and grass-stained knees. He seemed calmer, but he kept wetting his bed every night and he was strangely still, as if a light had gone out inside him.

The woman in charge of the older children kept encouraging Norah to participate in the organized activities. Part of Norah wanted to forget her troubles and run relay races and swim in the pool with the rest. But a kind of stubbornness had set in her, a mood that had always exasperated her mother — she called it her "black cloud" mood. When Norah felt like this she almost took pleasure in not enjoying or being grateful for what the grown-ups offered.

"You should join in more," Margery told her. "You'd like it here better if you did."

Norah knew she would, just as she knew she should be paying more attention to Gavin. But the black cloud engulfed her and she couldn't escape it.

The first day she squatted sullenly on the grass and watched a new game called baseball. There were new games, much more food and different accents. Still, it was difficult to believe she was really in Canada. Being here was much like being in the hostel in Liverpool: a tedious interlude of waiting for the next thing to happen.

The baseball bounced to a stop beside her. Norah threw it back and was suddenly gripped by a memory of bowling a cricket ball to her father — the sharp smell of newly cut grass and her father's encouraging, patient voice.

"Are you sure you don't want to play, Norah?" a woman asked kindly. Norah shook the memory out of her head as she refused.

After that she escaped from the daily activities by spending as much time as possible in the large room that had been stocked with children's books and set aside as a library. Norah had never been much of a reader. At school she was better at arithmetic than English, and at home there was too much to do outside to waste it on reading. But now she curled up with a book every day in one of the comfortable leather armchairs. Derek was always in there as well, along with several others. No one spoke; they were isolated like islands all over the room, each sheltering in a story.

The first book Norah picked out was called *Swallows and Amazons*. It was about a group of children who camped all by themselves on an island. They reminded her of the Skywatchers. The book was good and thick and lasted for three days. After she'd finished it, she found an even thicker one, *Swallowdale*, about the same children. She became so lost in their adventures that whenever the meal gong sounded she looked around, startled, as if she'd been a long way away.

One afternoon Miss Carmichael found her and shooed her outside. "It's too nice a day to be cooped up with a book. Come out to the grass. We're having a lovely time blowing bubbles and there are some journalists here who want to meet you all."

Reluctantly Norah put aside her book and followed Miss Carmichael to the lawn. She was handed a piece of bent wire and invited to dip it into a pail of sudsy water. Iridescent bubbles floated around her in the warm air. The weather was hot for September; the heat pressed on her skin like a wet sponge. Blinking, she watched her bubble rise, feeling like a mole who had emerged from under the ground.

Beside her, Lucy was being interviewed. "Now tell me what you think of Hitler," a journalist asked her.

"Hitler ith a nathty, nathty man," said Lucy coyly. Her lisp was newly acquired.

A family of five was being lined up for a picture. The star of the group was Johnnie, who posed in the middle of his older brothers and sisters. "We've come to Canada to help win the war," he declared proudly.

"Why do you say that?" a journalist prompted.

"'Cause children are a *nuisance* at home. If we're out of the way then the grown-ups can fight better!"

The journalists leaned forward eagerly. "Tell the nice people what you said on your first night when I asked how you were feeling," coaxed Miss Carmichael.

Johnnie looked confused until Miss Carmichael whispered to him. "I said — I said I was eager and brave!" he shouted. "I'm so brave I'll — I'll" — but his eldest sister dragged him away, her hand over his mouth.

Two women carrying cameras had been listening on the edge of the group. "Excuse me," one said to Miss Carmichael. "We're visiting Toronto from the United States and we couldn't help overhearing this adorable little boy. He's just too precious to be true! These children are evacuees, aren't they? How can we get one?"

"We don't call them evacuees," Miss Carmichael corrected. "That sounds as if they have no homes to return to. They are Canada's war guests. We're hosting them for the duration. If you want to sponsor a child you'll have to ask your own government."

The next day Miss Carmichael brought them the evening paper. Lucy's and Johnnie's pictures were included, among many others, over a story headed "Young British War Guests Blowing Peaceful Bubbles at Hart House".

"We'll have to send this home!" cried Dulcie. "Do you see how they put in your words, Lucy?"

Norah couldn't find herself or Gavin in the photographs. It made her feel more than ever that she wasn't really here.

IX

Alenoushka

Towards the end of the week the "nominated" children left to go to their friends and relatives. "Goodbye, Norah," said Dulcie hesitantly, as Miss Carmichael helped her carry her luggage to the door of Falconer House. "Do you think we'll see each other again?" She ran her tongue over her raw lips; her rash was worse.

"I'm sure you will," said Miss Carmichael. "The Milnes can find out from us where Norah is living, and there's going to be a party for all of you at Christmas."

Norah walked with Dulcie as far as the door and waved, surprised at feeling sad. Goosey and Loosey were a trial, but they were faces from home.

"When will Gavin and I go?" she asked Miss Carmichael that night. "Do you know who we'll be living with?"

"Not yet, but we'll match you up with someone as soon as possible. We need your beds for the next batch of children and school has already started. But don't worry, the response has been tremendous."

That was on Thursday. On Saturday, Norah heard her name mentioned as she came down the corridor to their room. Miss Carmichael was helping Mrs Ellis change the sheets.

"They've decided on a place for Norah and Gavin," Miss Carmichael was saying.

Norah froze and listened intently. She knew it was wrong to eavesdrop, but this was important. She couldn't catch the name Miss Carmichael gave in answer to Mrs Ellis's question.

"The family only wanted a boy," Miss Carmichael continued, "but they've persuaded them to take Norah as well. I do hope she'll settle in. Gavin is so sweet, but Norah can be difficult. She's such a loner, it isn't natural."

Norah was enraged. Gavin was the difficult one, not her! Did Miss Carmichael *enjoy* changing his sheets and washing out his pyjamas every day?

"I thought they'd be sent to the country," said Mrs Ellis. "They come from a small village, don't they?"

"I would have thought that would be more suitable, but apparently the woman was very specific about having as young a boy as possible — and Gavin's the only five-year-old left. I shouldn't be saying this, but I imagine they couldn't very well refuse her, she has so much money."

Norah shuffled her feet to let them know she was approaching.

"There you are, Norah!" Miss Carmichael smiled.

As with Mrs Pym, Norah had the feeling she felt sorry for her. "I have wonderful news! A family called Ogilvie would be delighted to have you and Gavin be their guests for the war. There are two ladies — Mrs Ogilvie, who's a widow, and her daughter. You'll be staying right here in Toronto — isn't that nice? You're lucky — the Ogilvies are very well off and you'll be living in a grand house in Rosedale. What do you think of that?"

It was far too much information to absorb at one time. Besides, the Ogilvies didn't want *her* — just Gavin. All Norah could say was, "When do we go?"

"Someone will pick you up tomorrow after lunch. Now come and help me pack your things."

Early Sunday morning the children were taken to church. The night before, Norah's dwindling group had been enlarged by a contingent of evacuees fresh from the ship. Norah felt sorry for them as they trooped out after supper for their medicals. At least she was finally leaving, however frightening her new home sounded.

In church the minister prayed for the British people "bravely carrying on their struggle alone." Norah prayed too, naming each member of her family carefully. She tried not to think of what they would be doing. Instead she imagined a family called Ogilvie; her chest grew heavy.

When they got back to Hart House they were told that a librarian had arrived to tell them stories before lunch.

"You take Gavin in," said Miss Carmichael. "I have all these new children to deal with."

Stories sounded babyish, but Norah took Gavin's hand and went into the room they used for recreation. Children were scattered all over, playing with toys and puzzles. A small woman with very bright eyes sat on a low stool in front of the fireplace, watching them calmly.

"Once upon a time there was a farmer and his wife who had one daughter, and she was courted by a gentleman . . . " she began slowly. Her vibrant voice cut through the chatter. As she carried on, the children drew closer and squatted on the floor in front of her.

When she reached the point where the people in the story were all wailing in the cellar, some of the children began to smile. By the time the man was trying to jump into his trousers, they were giggling. Gavin laughed for the first time since they'd left England, and Norah felt a chuckle rise inside her.

" . . . and that was the story of 'The Three Sillies', " the woman concluded.

"Tell us another!" demanded a fat little girl called Emma.

"Once upon a time Henny Penny was picking up corn when — whack! — an acorn fell on her head. 'Goodness, gracious me!' said Henny Penny. 'The sky is falling! I must go and tell the king.' "

She came to the part about "Goosey Loosey" and Norah grinned, looking around for Dulcie. Then she remembered she had gone.

There was a satisfied silence in the room after Foxy
Loxy had finished off his witless victims. "Of course,
the sky wasn't *really* falling," said Emma knowingly.

"It is at home!" declared Johnnie. "It's falling down
all over England, and that's why we had to go away."

The librarian looked startled, but only for a
second. She showed them how to do a game with their
fingers called "Piggy Wig and Piggy Wee." Then she
told them "The Three Little Pigs". All the younger children huffed and puffed with the wolf, even Gavin.
They moved closer to her and one of them stroked her
shoes. Emma wriggled onto her knee.

"And now, I want to tell you the story of
Alenoushka and her brother." Her tone had become
sad and solemn and the rollicking atmosphere changed
to hushed expectancy. "Once upon a time there were
two orphan children, a little boy and a little girl. Their
father and mother were dead and they were all alone.
The little boy was called Ivanoushka and the little girl's
name was Alenoushka. They set out together to walk
through the whole of the great wide world. It was a
long journey they set out on, and they did not think of
any end to it, but only of moving on and on . . . "

The back of Norah's neck prickled. She was pulled
into the story as if by a magnet and she *became*
Alenoushka, trying to stop her little brother from
drinking water from the hoofprints of animals, and
desperate when he did and turned into a little lamb.

The other children were as spellbound as she.
They sat like stones while the rich voice went on,

forgetting the storyteller in their utter absorption in the story itself.

> O my brother Ivanoushka,
> A heavy stone is round my throat,
> Silken grass grows through my fingers,
> Yellow sand lies on my breast.

Norah didn't realize her eyes had welled with tears until one rolled down her cheek.

The story ended happily. Alenoushka was rescued from a witch's spell, and when she threw her arms around the lamb he became her brother once more. "And they all lived happily together and ate honey every day, with white bread and new milk."

The haunting voice stopped and the room was still. Norah's body was loose and relaxed. She felt the rough rug under her legs and Gavin's warm thigh pressing against hers.

The librarian stood up and left the room without acknowledging them or saying goodbye. It was as if the stories had used her to tell themselves. The children got up quietly and went in to lunch.

Norah's ease ended after they'd eaten. She and Gavin, dressed in cleaned and pressed clothes, waited in the front hall.

"Where are we going to live *now*?" whispered Gavin.

Norah was struggling to secure her hair-slide.

"What do you mean, silly? We haven't lived anywhere yet."

"Yes, we have. First we lived in the hostel. Then we lived on the boat with Mrs Pym and then we lived here with Miss Carmichael. Now where are we going to live?"

"With a family called Ogilvie who have a posh house. You know that, Gavin, we've already told you."

Miss Carmichael came up to say goodbye. "Now, be sure to behave like polite guests and everything will be fine. Someone will come and visit you in a while to see how you're getting along."

The front door opened and into the hall stepped a plain, plump woman. She wore a brown linen suit and a beige hat; her beige hair was twisted into a tidy knot and her brown eyes looked anxious. "How do you do? I am Miss Ogilvie. And this must be Norah and Gavin. I'm very pleased to meet you both." Her voice sounded more frightened than pleased.

Norah shook the woman's limp hand. It was covered with a spotless beige glove.

"I want to stay here," whimpered Gavin, hiding behind Miss Carmichael.

"Off you go, Gavin." She handed him a large boiled sweet. This was such a surprise that Gavin sucked it busily instead of crying.

Miss Carmichael kissed them both. "I'll see you at the Christmas party," she smiled.

Miss Ogilvie led them out to a sleek grey car. "Perhaps you'd prefer to sit beside each other in the back," she said hesitantly.

Norah watched the university become smaller and smaller behind them. Then she turned around and watched the neat back of Miss Ogilvie's hair as they drove wordlessly through the still Sunday streets to their new home.

Part Two

X

The Ogilvies

The car turned into a quiet, leafy street and stopped at the house at the end, a house so tall and enormous it looked like a red brick castle. There was even a tower. The windows stared down at Norah like a crowd of inquisitive eyes. She carried her suitcase up wide white steps flanked by green pillars.

Inside, the house was even more resplendent. The front hall was as large as two rooms in Little Whitebull. It looked even bigger because it was almost empty of furniture, except for a mahogany table on one side with a silver bowl full of roses on it. Arched doorways led to several rooms off the hall; a curved staircase disappeared upwards.

Miss Ogilvie stood in the hall beside them as if she, too, were a stranger who didn't know what to do next. "Now, let's see . . . " Her timid voice rang out in the silence. "Mother is anxious to meet you, of course, but this is her rest time. I'll show you your room and you can unpack before tea."

She led them up two levels, first on thickly carpeted stairs, then on bare, slippery ones. At the very top there were only two rooms: a small one containing a huge bathtub and a large, circular bedroom with built-in seats around its windowed walls.

"This is the tower!" cried Norah. She ran to the windows and looked out at the lush tops of trees.

"Yes . . . I hope you don't mind being up here alone. Is it all right?" Miss Ogilvie's voice was shy. "I prepared it myself."

Norah had never encountered a grown-up who was so nervous. She walked around the room carefully, trying not to make sudden movements that might startle her.

Two narrow beds were along one wall, each covered in a satin eiderdown. New-looking curtains hung from the windows. On a table were piled boxes of jigsaw puzzles and games. Some battered tin cars and trucks were parked in a row under the table and a shabby rocking horse with a real horsehair mane stood in a corner. Gavin went over to it and stroked the mane gently.

"I'm afraid they're mostly boys' things," Miss Ogilvie apologized. "You see . . . " Her voice faltered.

Norah thought she was about to reveal they had only wanted a boy. Her excitement over the lofty room subsided.

" . . . you see, this was our nursery — my

brother's and mine. Most of these toys belonged to him, but I found one of my dolls for you, Norah." She pointed to a small doll with a chipped plaster face lying on one of the beds. "I used to love dolls, but of course not all girls do," the soft voice continued anxiously.

Norah fingered the doll's yellowed eyelet dress. Miss Ogilvie watched so hopefully that she tried to sound enthusiastic. "Thank you. She's very nice. Where's your brother, then? Does he still live here?"

The woman's plain face seemed to collapse upon itself. "Oh, no! Hugh was killed in the war. Not this war, the first one."

"Oh. I'm sorry."

There seemed nothing more to say after that. Miss Ogilvie looked as if she wanted to leave. "You get yourselves settled," she said, "and I'll come up for you when it's time for tea. We have a formal tea on Sundays and an informal supper later. Perhaps you could change into your best clothes. And could you wipe his mouth?" she added hesitantly. Gavin's lips were smeared red from the sweet Miss Carmichael had given him. "First impressions are important, don't you think? I'll see you later." She disappeared down the stairs.

The horse creaked as Gavin rocked on it slowly. Norah took out all their clothes and put them away in the wardrobe and the chest of drawers. There was lots of space left over when she'd finished. She placed the photograph of the family on the small table between the beds. At the bottom of her case she found her bundle of shrapnel and ran her hands over the smooth, iridescent metal before she decided to hide it under her mattress.

Then she made Gavin wash his face and go to the toilet. That was in with the bathtub; at home it was a separate room attached to the scullery. She had already become used to pressing a handle instead of pulling a chain.

She picked out some clothes for them. The only dress she had that was fancier than the one she wore was a very rumpled winter one of flowered Viyella. She tried to get rid of the wrinkles with a wet flannel.

"I'm too hot," complained Gavin, after Norah had made him put on his grey wool shorts and knitted waistcoat. At least the waistcoat partly covered up his wrinkled white shirt.

"Stop whining. You heard what she said about first impressions." Norah looked for a ribbon and tied a sloppy bow on one side of her head. Even the ribbon was wrinkled.

"Let's take these horrid things off." She unfastened the identification disks around their necks and threw them into the wastepaper basket, feeling lighter.

They sat quietly on the window seat and looked down on the rooftops below them. Norah began to feel hopeful. Perhaps it wouldn't be so bad, living here. Even if the Ogilvies only wanted Gavin, this marvellous room was an unexpected pleasure. And if she were as polite as possible, they might want her as well.

Miss Ogilvie knocked at their door. "Oh," she gulped, as she inspected them. "You should have asked the maid to iron your clothes. Never mind, it's too late now. Mother likes people to be punctual and she's already waiting in the den."

She acted as if they were about to be greeted by royalty. Norah's chest felt constricted as she and Gavin descended the long staircase and followed Miss Ogilvie into a room off the hall.

"Come in, come in," a resonant voice called impatiently. "Let's have a look at you."

In contrast to the stark hall, the cosy room overflowed with fat chintz chairs, more bowls of flowers and tables crowded with ornaments and silver-framed photographs. "Den" was a suitable word; it was like stepping into a scented, muggy cave.

The voice had come from a woman reclining in a chair by the window. Her full face was circled by a thatch of curly silver hair. Her wide grey eyes almost matched her hair. An ample bosom swelled under her red silk dress, like the breast of a well-fed robin. In contrast to her stout body, the long legs which stretched out on the Persian carpet were slim and elegant.

"Come and shake hands," commanded Mrs Ogilvie. Norah shrank from the extended fingers, but she had to take them. A ring with sharp stones bit into her own wet palm.

"You must be Norah — and this is little Gavin, of course. Do sit down. I'm delighted to meet you both."

Mrs Ogilvie assumed they knew who *she* was. Norah sat, waiting for her next instructions. A throbbing energy came from the woman, as if she were an engine running in perfect order. No wonder her daughter was so pale and subdued; her mother seemed to have sucked all the colour from her.

Gavin gazed at Mrs Ogilvie's splendour as if he were bewitched. Mrs Ogilvie looked him over and purred with pleasure. "Aren't *you* a handsome little boy! You come over here by me." She pulled a low stool close to her feet. "I won't eat you! You and I are going to be great friends."

Gavin advanced slowly, his eyes never leaving her face. One hand burrowed in his pocket.

"You're five, aren't you. And what do you have in your pocket?"

"Creature," whispered Gavin, pulling out the elephant to show her.

"Creature! What a charming name! Look what I have for you and Creature." She opened a drawer in the table beside her and took out a small tin aeroplane. "There! *I* know what little boys like."

Gavin stroked the aeroplane with shining eyes. Norah gazed at it jealously. It was a very good model of a Blenheim. She wondered if she would get a present too. "Say thank you," she hissed.

"Now, now let him be," admonished Mrs Ogilvie. "This is a new and strange experience for him." She looked at Norah again. "What part of England was it that you're from?"

"Kent," mumbled Norah. She offered a few details about the village when Miss Ogilvie questioned her. Mrs Ogilvie had immediately turned her attention back to Gavin, who was telling her about the ship. Norah shifted irritably. How could he talk so easily to a stranger when he had hardly talked to his own sister the whole trip?

"How frightening it must have been when the German planes flew over," shuddered Miss Ogilvie. "You must be so relieved to be safe."

"*I* wasn't frightened," declared Norah, still watching Gavin. "I didn't *want* to be safe."

Mrs Ogilvie looked over and frowned. "She's awfully small for her age, Mary. Are you sure she's ten?"

"I'm ten and a *half*," said Norah indignantly. "You needn't speak as if I wasn't here."

Miss Ogilvie gasped. Norah regretted her words when she saw Mrs Ogilvie's expression.

"Sauce! We won't have rudeness in *this* house, my girl."

Norah knew she should apologize, but something in those determined grey eyes made her want to be just as stubborn back. She sat in angry silence, all her resolutions to be polite flown away.

Mrs Ogilvie waited for a few seconds, then she gave a knowing glance at her daughter. She picked up a little brass bell and rang it.

A maid in a ruffled white apron wheeled in a trolley with an elaborate tea on it: egg sandwiches and chicken sandwiches, warm scones with butter and raspberry jam, thin lemon biscuits and a heavy spice cake blanketed with maple icing. Norah ate rapidly. It was tricky to balance everything on her knee; she finally copied Gavin and squatted on the floor. Mrs Ogilvie made them drink milk. "Tea's not good for children," she said when Gavin asked for some.

"Now, let's get ourselves organized," she said, setting down the silver teapot. "I thought you might feel more comfortable if you called me Aunt Florence and my daughter Aunt Mary. I know you'll feel at home here — we follow the good old British traditions. And in this terrible war, especially, we're eager to help our mother country as much as we can. That's why I decided to take on war guests — to do my part." She looked at Norah as if she expected her to be profoundly grateful, then smiled at Gavin. "And, of course, I wanted to have a little one around again." Turning back to Norah, she continued. "You will have to do your part, too. I expect you to be quiet, clean and well mannered. You'll be treated like members of the family, and I'm sure your parents will be glad to learn you've come to such a good home. Do you have any questions?"

"No," muttered Norah.

"No, what?"

"No . . . Aunt Florence." The name stuck in her throat like dry crumbs. Why should she have to call someone "aunt" who wasn't even related to her? Then she remembered she did have a question. "What about . . . school?" That was a hurdle she wasn't at all prepared for, but she had to find out about it sometime.

"You'll begin school on Tuesday. The people at Hart House suggested you stay home for a day first to get used to your new family."

The maid arrived back and removed the trolley. Then there was an awkward silence. Norah pushed up her sleeves; her winter dress made her feel hot in the stuffy room.

"Well, now, what shall we do next?" Aunt Florence smiled kindly, but Norah only looked at the carpet. "Why don't you have a game of cribbage with Norah, Mary, and Gavin and I will play fish."

Her daughter obediently rose and led Norah to a table in the corner. On it lay a long narrow board with ivory pegs stuck in its holes, a pack of cards and some paper and pencils. Norah tried to pay attention as Aunt Mary taught her the game, but she couldn't help listening to Gavin's gleeful voice as he ordered "Fish!" again and again.

Cribbage was so confusing that she was relieved when Aunt Florence finally told them to go back to their room. "When Mary fetches you, you can have a light supper in the kitchen. Sunday is our bridge night, and I'd like you to come in and meet everyone." She dismissed them with a regal wave of her arm.

"Aunt Florence is beautiful!" said Gavin when they were back in the tower. "Do you think she's the Queen of Canada?"

Norah scowled. "Don't be such an idiot, of course she's not. And how can you possibly like her? She's mean and bossy and *fat*."

"Oh." Gavin looked deflated. "Does that mean we aren't going to stay here, if you don't like her?"

"Do you think it's up to me? If it was, we'd never have left England! Of course we're staying. There's nowhere else to go."

Gavin climbed onto the horse and hummed, zooming his plane in the air. "Creature thinks he might *like* to stay here."

Aunt Mary came up at six-thirty and told them to get into their pyjamas. Norah wanted to protest about getting ready for bed so early, but she knew that anything she said to Aunt Mary would just make her all the more nervous. They put on their dressing gowns and slippers and followed her down to the kitchen.

Aunt Mary left them with the cook, Mrs Hancock. She was an older, good-natured woman with red hands and untidy hair she kept pushing under a hairnet. "All the way from England you've come!" she marvelled. "I've always wanted to visit the old country. I saw the King and Queen when they visited Canada last year. Real close they were, I could have touched them. Sit down here and try my tomato soup."

They ate soup, toast and pudding at a scrubbed pine table. The kitchen was much like theirs at home, except it had a large refrigerator and no fireplace. Mrs Hancock was comfortable to talk to. She showed them how the refrigerator made its own ice cubes.

"Call me Hanny," she said. "Everyone in the family always has. This is just like the old days, when Mary and Hughie used to eat their Sunday supper in here. That must be thirty years ago! What a treat to have young ones in the house, isn't it Edith?"

Edith, the maid, who was slouched over a novel at the other end of the table, ignored Hanny's comment. "It's my evening off. How soon can I leave?" she asked sulkily.

"Not until you carry in their sandwiches. Have some more pudding, Gavin."

Norah was sorry to leave the kitchen when Aunt Mary fetched them again. She led them to the door of the living room. At one end of it, seven adults were sitting around two square tables. Mrs Ogilvie looked up from a pack of cards she was shuffling expertly. "Here are our young war guests! Come in and meet everyone."

All the adults got up and moved towards the children with broad smiles and outstretched hands. Norah's hair was ruffled and her arm pumped vigorously. "How do you do?" "Welcome to Canada!" "Where do you live in England?" "Did you have a good voyage?" "Are you beginning to feel settled?"

Since it was impossible to answer so many questions, Norah kept silent. When Gavin began to talk timidly about Creature the adult voices froze.

"What a darling accent!" one woman cooed when he'd finished. Norah frowned – didn't Canadians realize *they* were the ones with accents?

"And what do you think of Canada, Norah?" a man asked. "Is it very different from England?"

Once again there was an expectant hush. Norah stared at the beaming faces and blurted out the first words that came to her. "Everyone in Canada has very white teeth."

The adults roared with laughter and Norah blushed with confusion. What had she said that was so funny?

"Off to bed with you now," said Aunt Florence. She kissed Gavin and began to approach Norah but when Norah backed away she changed her mind. "And turn out your lights at once. You must both be very tired."

They were sent back upstairs by themselves. "Creature understands now," said Gavin when they were in bed. "We're going to live here for a long time, until I'm eight, and then we're going to live with Muv and Dad again."

"Not until you're eight! Maybe almost seven."

"Miss Carmichael said eight."

"Well, she's wrong! Dad said 'perhaps a year'. Those were his *exact* words."

Gavin soon fell asleep. Norah tossed for a while, then got up and sat on the window seat. A warm wind had risen — it turned the trees into a surging leafy sea. Rosedale was much quieter than the university. Occasionally a car passed or a dog barked, but in between all she could hear was the steady burr of some insect. It wasn't quite dark, much too early to go to sleep. Norah stared out the window with a sad finality.

This was it, then, their home for the duration, however long that might be. The war and England seemed far away from the cushioned luxury of the Ogilvies' life — their life, now.

She noticed that there was a hinge along the back of the window seat, and when she lifted it up she found a cavity stuffed with blankets. That would be a better hiding place for her shrapnel. After she'd placed it there, she got her coat and uncovered the five pounds Mum had sewn in the lining. She hid it under the blankets as well and closed the lid. Mum and Dad had told her to give the money to her new family for safekeeping, but Norah decided she would rather have it close at hand — just in case.

She got back into bed and thought of her abandoned room at home, with her parents sleeping below. She began to cry softly, but even that seemed useless, so she lay and listened to the night until her eyes closed.

XI

Monday

Breakfast was a formal meal in the dining room. Norah and Gavin and Aunt Mary sat at one end of a long polished table, eating the porridge and eggs and bacon that Hanny brought in. "Mother never gets up for breakfast," Aunt Mary explained. She seemed more relaxed without her mother.

In front of each plate was a piece of long yellow fruit. "What's this?" asked Gavin.

"It's a banana, silly," Norah told him. "We haven't had bananas since before the war," she explained to Aunt Mary. "He doesn't remember."

"Ouch!" Gavin had bitten into the skin without peeling it.

"You poor child — let me help." Aunt Mary showed him how to take off the skin. "Now, what would you like to do today? We should think of something nice before you start school tomorrow, Norah."

"And Gavin," Norah added.

"Isn't Gavin too young for school? I thought he was five. I suppose he could go to kindergarten, but I think Mother would rather have him at home . . . ."

"He'll be six in November and anyway, he's already been to school. He was in the Infants last year. So he's old enough, aren't you Gavin?" Norah felt proud of her brother this morning; for the first time since the hostel, he hadn't wet the bed.

"I don't think Mother knows he's almost six," said Aunt Mary doubtfully. "I'll have to tell her, I suppose."

"I don't like school," said Gavin.

"You did after you learned to do up your buttons," Norah reminded him. Gavin used to come crying to her at playtime after he'd been to the lav, and she'd have to button up his trousers behind a tree. Thinking of that made her resent him again; she would have to look after him even more at a new Canadian school.

"Your school is only six blocks away," Aunt Mary was saying. "I found out at church yesterday that you'll have some friends from England there — the Smith girls. They and their brother are war guests of our minister, Reverend Milne."

Norah put down her spoon. She had forgotten about Dulcie and Lucy. It seemed odd to associate them with the Ogilvies.

"Would you like to invite them for lunch?" asked Aunt Mary. "They haven't started school either and Mrs Milne decided to keep them home today so you could all begin together."

"No, thank you." Norah tried not to sound rude.

"Could I — could I just go out for a walk instead?"

"All by yourself? I wonder what Mother would say." Aunt Mary looked at Norah's pleading face. "I suppose it's all right. Everyone in the neighbourhood knows who we are, so if you get lost just knock on someone's door. Don't go too far, though, and wear your hat. I'll expect you back in an hour."

Norah tried to be still enough to listen to the rest of Aunt Mary's cautious directions. Then she dashed up-stairs to use the toilet and fetch her hat.

On the way down, she paused on the landing outside Aunt Florence's bedroom. Despite her impa-tience to be out, she couldn't help stopping to listen when she heard a voice. She was doing a lot of eaves-dropping these days, but it seemed the only way to get information.

Aunt Florence couldn't be talking to herself. She must have a telephone in there. Norah had never heard of anyone having a telephone in her bedroom. In Ring-den, the only people who had one at all were the doc-tor, the policeman and Mrs Chandler; the rest of them used the call box on the main street.

"The girl?" said the throaty voice. "Well, she's cheeky, but we'll work on that. Girls are so sly — I had to be much stricter with Mary than I was with Hugh. But wait until you see Gavin! He's such a character, with an adorable accent. And such rosy cheeks! The girl is thin and pale — you'd never guess they were brother and sister. And their clothes . . . well, you can see they're not well off. I'm going to take Gavin shopping tomorrow. With his fair colouring, he'd look so fetching in a navy-blue sailor suit. Would they still carry them at Holt's, do you think? It's been so long since I've bought children's clothes. I'm telling you, Audrey, this is all making me feel young again."

Aunt Florence wouldn't be able to take Gavin shopping when she found out he'd be in school tomorrow, Norah thought as she continued down the stairs.

As soon as she stepped outside, she forgot her resentment. A delicious sensation of freedom swept through her. It was the first time since the day she'd left England that she could go where she pleased. And it was the first time since the war began that she'd gone out with nothing to carry — no gas mask, identity card or lifebelt.

She left her hat on the steps and walked along the sidewalk slowly, savouring the sun on her bare arms and legs. It was going to be a scorcher, Hanny had told them, but the morning air was still fresh. The winding street divided around islands of flowers. Ranged along it were houses as grand and impassive as the Ogilvies', some of brick and some of stone. Norah wondered why none of them had names. In one she saw a curtain twitch, as if someone had peeked out at her.

The twisting streets were like a maze. Norah noted each turn carefully so she wouldn't get lost. She was proud of herself when she found her way back to the Ogilvies'. Then she went around again the other way. At one house a small, wiry dog rushed up to her from behind a wrought iron fence. When she crouched down it licked her fingers, pushing its nose through the railings.

After she'd completed the circle again, it didn't seem like an hour yet, and she didn't feel like leaving the bright outdoors for the Ogilvies' dim house. Their garden was tiny; it seemed odd to have such a large house on such a small property. But there was something much better than a garden behind the house: a thick patch of trees that spilled down the bank into a valley.

Norah plunged into the trees, thrusting through bushes and pushing aside branches, until she reached a clearing at the bottom. High above her stretched a bridge; she could hear the rumble of cars driving over it. Someone had written rude words on one of the concrete supports.

You could make a good fort here; but it would be lonely to build a fort all by herself and she felt too lazy to start. She sat on a log and scraped the ground with a twig. When she thought of school tomorrow her chest felt heavy, but she breathed deeply and scratched pictures in the dirt of all the aeroplanes she knew.

When she had been there for a long while Norah suddenly remembered the time. She scrambled up the bank and rushed into the Ogilvies' house. For a second she almost thought she was at home, for from the den came a familiar voice: "This is the BBC news coming to you directly from London." She paused outside the door; would Aunt Florence be angry?

The Ogilvies were sitting around a large wireless. Aunt Florence switched it off quickly as soon as she saw Norah — as if she didn't want her to hear. "Where have you *been*, young lady? We were just about to call the police!"

"Out for a walk," Norah mumbled. She raised her head and tossed back her hair defiantly. "Aunt Mary said I could."

"She said you had gone around the block, but you've been away for hours! And just look at you — you're covered in leaves and dirt. Where have you been? You've scared us half to death. If I had been consulted, you wouldn't have been allowed out alone at all!"

"I went into the woods behind the garden and I forgot about the time." Aunt Mary looked so stricken that Norah added, "I'm sorry."

"You went into the *ravine*?" said Aunt Florence crisply. "This won't do, my girl! The ravine attracts rough boys and it's muddy and dangerous. You are never to go there again, do you understand? Get yourself cleaned up for lunch."

As Norah shook out her twig-covered dress and changed her dusty socks, she resolved to go back to her secret place in the ravine as soon as she could. She would just have to be careful not to get caught.

The rest of Monday crept by so slowly, that Norah thought she would burst with boredom. Aunt Mary suggested a drive, but her mother said it was too hot. All afternoon they sat listlessly on a screened verandah at the back of the house, sipping lemonade. Norah lay on the floor beside Gavin, helping him construct houses out of cards. She thought longingly of *Swallow-dale*, which she'd had to leave unfinished at Hart House. Then she remembered Aunt Mary pointing out a bookcase in their room. Could she just leave and go up there by herself — as if she were at home?

"Excuse me," she mumbled. "I'm going to my room."

"Of course, Norah." Aunt Mary smiled at her. Aunt Florence didn't even look up from her needlepoint. She had been sulking ever since Mary had told her that Gavin would have to go to school.

Norah decided to explore the house first. No one had offered to show her around, but she could see it for herself while the Ogilvies were safely on the verandah and Hanny was off.

She wondered why two people needed so many rooms. On the main floor, behind the den, she found another room, with a photograph of a sober-faced, whiskered gentleman on the desk: Mr Ogilvie, she decided. Upstairs were five bedrooms, connected by spacious halls covered in slippery rugs. The rooms were crammed with dark furniture. They smelled stale and their heavy curtains were pulled tight against the sun. Aunt Florence's and Aunt Mary's doors were firmly closed.

She found a set of back stairs leading up from the kitchen. When she put her head around a curtain at the top, she gasped. Edith was stretched out on a cot with her stockings off, fanning herself with a folded paper. She sat up and shouted at Norah, "What do you think you're doing, poking your nose up here! Get away!"

Norah scuttled down the stairs, through the kitchen and hall, and up the other staircase to the tower. She collapsed on her bed, her heart hammering. She knew that Hanny came in to work every day; she hadn't realized that Edith lived right in the house. From the brief glance she'd had at her room, it looked smaller and barer than any of the unused ones.

The tower was hot, but Norah decided it was the best room in the house. When she'd caught her breath she examined the books. Most of them were old schoolbooks; there was nothing by the man who wrote *Swallowdale*. The only story she found was called *Elsie Dinsmore*. Its spongy pages were spotted with mildew; "Mary Ogilvie" was written on the flyleaf in careful round handwriting. It was a strange book, about a repulsively good little girl who was very religious. Norah struggled along with it until dinner.

That evening Norah had a telephone call. "For me?" she asked with disbelief. Who knew her in Canada?

"Hello, Norah, this is Dulcie!" said the high, nervous voice.

"Hello, Dulcie," said Norah without enthusiasm. Still, it cheered her up to hear someone familiar.

"Isn't it super that we live in the same neighbourhood? The Milnes are ever so nice. We've had a holiday since we arrived. What I was wondering was . . . do you think we could try to sit next to each other at school tomorrow? It's quite a large school, Aunt Dorothy says . . . "

What she was really asking was if they could stick

together as if they were friends. The Smiths had only come to Ringden two years ago. Norah remembered how scared Dulcie had looked on her first day of school and how the other children had taken advantage of this to tease her.

Norah had never been a new girl. She had always been one of the most popular people in her class — surely that would carry on. It was flattering that Dulcie recognized her superior position.

"I'll see what I can do," she said grandly.

"Oh, thank you, Norah!" said Dulcie. "See you tomorrow!"

Aunt Florence came into the hall. "Off to bed with you, now," she said briskly. "You and Gavin have a big day tomorrow. I don't know how that delicate little boy is going to bear it."

XII

"Now in School and Liking It"

As if Aunt Florence had willed it, Gavin woke up the next morning too sick to go to school. His nose streamed, he had a croaky cough and his forehead was hot.

Aunt Florence moved him downstairs into the bedroom opposite hers and settled him against lofty pillows under a mountain of blankets. When Norah left with Aunt Mary she could hear the rich voice coaxing, "Would you like me to read *Winnie-the-Pooh* to you? I once knew a little boy who loved that story."

The walk to Prince Edward School was not long; they reached the two-storey red brick building much sooner than Norah wished. She tried not to flinch from the curious stares of the children standing around in noisy groups. Aunt Mary took her inside to look for the headmaster; she called him the "principal".

The principal's secretary told them to wait in the

outer office. They sat on a hard bench and listened to a deep voice talking on the telephone from behind a frosted glass door. Soon Dulcie and Lucy bounced up, accompanied by a complacent-looking, smiling woman.

"Good morning, Miss Ogilvie," she said. "This must be Norah. I'm so pleased that Dulcie and Lucy will have friends from home. But where's your little brother?"

Aunt Mary explained about Gavin. Mrs Milne introduced her to the Smiths and said that Derek was going to high school. "He's such a clever boy, they've put him ahead a year. Isn't it a privilege to have the care of these children, Miss Ogilvie? The Reverend and I didn't realize how empty our lives were until they came. Already I feel as if they are part of the family." She plumped the bow in Lucy's hair and kissed her fondly.

"Mr Evans would like to talk to the ladies first," interrupted the secretary. She led Aunt Mary and Mrs Milne behind the glass door and then left the office. "You wait here quietly," she told the children. "He'll see you in a few minutes."

"Miss Ogilvie seems very nice," said Dulcie. Her rash, like Lucy's lisp, had disappeared. "What's *Mrs* Ogilvie like? Uncle Cedric says she's a dragon, but a pillar of support for the church."

Norah shrugged. She couldn't think of any words to describe Aunt Florence, although "dragon" and "pillar" certainly seemed right.

"Aunt Dorothy and Uncle Cedric aren't at all strict,"

said Lucy, trying to balance on one leg. "They let us do whatever we want and they've taken us to all sorts of interesting places. Have you been on a streetcar, yet, Norah? Have you seen the Toronto Islands and Casa Loma? *We* have."

"Isn't it odd how they shop for food here?" Dulcie giggled. "Everything in one store! Does your house have a refrigerator? Ours does, and we can have as much water as we like in the bath. Do stop that, Lucy, we're supposed to be sitting quietly."

Goosey and Loosey babbled on and Norah only half-listened; she kept her eyes on the glass door. At home the headmaster — *principal*, she corrected herself — was also her teacher. He didn't have an office or a secretary, or a mysterious glass door.

"It's an enormous school, isn't it?" said Dulcie. "Aunt Dorothy says it goes up to age fourteen!"

In the village school their age group had been the oldest. As Norah contemplated this, the glass door opened a crack. "Come in, girls," called Mrs Milne.

They stood in a row in front of the principal's desk. He leaned across it and shook their hands. "Welcome to Canada," he said vaguely. He was a sleepy-looking man who seemed preoccupied, as if none of them were really in the room with him.

"Yes, um, war guests — there are already twenty-four in the school and they're settling in well. We're glad that Canada has been able to help you at this difficult time. Now, about your grade levels." He told them that Lucy would be in grade two, and Norah and Dulcie in grade five. "Say goodbye to your guardians now and I'll take you to your classrooms."

"I'll meet you at the front door at 12:30," whispered Aunt Mary.

The three girls followed Mr Evans's back down the hall. The wooden floor made their footsteps echo loudly. Everyone else was already in class. Norah and Dulcie waited outside while the principal took Lucy by the hand into a room labelled Two B — Mrs Newbery. Then he continued to a door that said Five A — Miss Liers.

He knocked before poking in his head. "Miss Liers, your war guests — Dulcie Smith and Norah Stoakes." They stepped through the doorway and he closed them in.

Miss Liers was a thin, bitter-looking woman with dark hair scraped back so tightly in a bun that it pulled on her skin. Although her words were kind, her tone was sarcastic, as if they had done something wrong. "How do you do, Dulcie and Norah? We've been expecting you. I've given you desks next to each other over there. Five A is proud to have some war guests. We felt deprived without any, didn't we, class?"

Five A stared at Norah and Dulcie as if the multitude of eyes were one big eye.

Miss Liers handed them each some pencils and notebooks, continuing to talk in a strained, cold voice. Why did she resent them? Norah wondered, lifting up the lid of her desk to hide from all those eyes. She found out at once.

"Dulcie and Norah are extremely lucky," Miss Liers was saying. "*All* British evacuees are lucky that Canada has invited them here for the duration. But we mustn't forget that there are other children in Europe who aren't so lucky. Little Belgian and Dutch and Jewish children whose circumstances are far graver than British children's. Let us hope that our government will act to bring those children over to safety as well."

She paused expectantly and the class droned, "Yes, Miss Liers." But no one was listening. They were all peeking at the two new girls.

Norah bent her head over her arithmetic book as the interrupted lesson continued. It wasn't her fault she had been sent to Canada instead of a European child. Perhaps she could tell Miss Liers sometime that she would have been happy if one could have been evacuated in her place.

She discovered quickly that the problems were ones she had done last year. Beside her, Dulcie gave a small sigh of relief. Arithmetic had been her weakest subject.

Miss Liers didn't call on either of them. When some of the pupils went to the blackboard to write down their answers, Norah felt safe enough to raise her head and examine the room.

It was as large as their whole school in Ringden. The five rows of desks had wide spaces between them and at one end there was a raised platform with a piano on it. The walls were hung with rolled-up maps and a picture of the Royal Family, just like at home. Norah's desk was beside high windows; she could see out to the houses across the street.

Next she looked at the pupils. Everyone was too busy concentrating to return her stare. They didn't *seem* any different from English children, but there were so many of them. In Ringden there had been only thirty-two children divided into two age groups. Here there were — she counted quickly — twenty-seven, including her and Dulcie, and everyone seemed to be the same age. If there were two rooms for each of the eight grades, there were over five hundred children in the school!

A loud bell interrupted Norah's private arithmetic. She looked around to see what they were supposed to do next. All the children put down their pencils and sat up alertly.

"Before you go out for recess, I want two volunteers to look after our war guests," said Miss Liers.

All the girls shot up their arms. One large, smart-alecky boy with red hair waved his wildly, while his friends hooted and cheered.

"That will do, Charlie!" There was instant silence; Miss Liers commanded respect.

"Babs Miller will look after Dulcie, and Ernestine Gagnon, Norah. Show them where to go and what to do for the next few days. Make them feel at home here."

Babs Miller started asking Dulcie eager questions as soon as they were allowed to talk. Ernestine looked longingly after Dulcie as they left the room, as if she had wanted her instead of Norah. She was a very pretty girl with glossy brown curls held back with a huge bow.

Norah was desperate for a toilet. "Where's the lav?" she asked, as she and Ernestine started out to the playground.

"The lav? What's that?"

Oh, help — what would they call it? At the Ogilvies' they said "bathroom", but surely there weren't any rooms with baths in them at school.

"The WC," Norah tried next.

"The WC? Are you asking riddles or something?" Ernestine looked annoyed, as they stood inside the door and everyone surged past.

"The — the *toilet!*" burst out Norah, flushing with embarrassment.

"Oh, the *washroom* — why didn't you say so? Follow me." Looking even angrier, Ernestine led her to a large room with a long row of cubicles in the basement. Norah had to stay there awhile. By the time Ernestine had waited for her and taken her out to the playground, recess was almost over.

The boys and girls seemed to have separate play areas. Ernestine and Norah went up to the grade five girls, all standing around Dulcie in an eager crowd.

"How long did it take you to get over?"

"What was it like on the ship?"

Dulcie beamed at all this unusual attention. "The ship was *scary,*" she said importantly. "Some other girls and I started a club to keep up our courage."

"I love your dress, Dulcie," said Ernestine, pushing past Norah and forgetting her.

Norah assessed the situation quickly. This would never do — Dulcie was the one who was supposed to be unpopular! And she wasn't describing any of the interesting parts. Norah opened her mouth to tell someone about the German plane, but another bell clanged and they all swept past her to line up at the girls' entrance.

Very well, then, she thought angrily. If they were going to like Goosey better than her, she would not tell them anything. "You come from the same village as Dulcie, don't you?" asked the girl in front of her. Norah mumbled "Mmmm," and looked the other way.

For the rest of the morning Norah returned any friendly looks she received with proud reserve. She glanced at the picture of Princess Margaret Rose, standing regally in her Coronation robe beside her sister and parents. Norah pretended she was a princess as well, too elevated to mix with Canadian children.

During English, Miss Liers read them a poem called "How They Brought the Good News from Ghent to Aix". Norah listened intently. It was the first poem she'd ever liked, about the kind of noble deed the Skywatchers would do. Miss Liers asked her to read the first verse again. Norah stood up and recited it in a fierce, animated voice:

> I sprang to the stirrup, and Joris, and he;
> I galloped, Dirck galloped, we galloped all three;
> "Good speed!" cried the watch, as the gate-bolts
>   undrew;
> "Speed!" echoed the wall to us galloping through;
> Behind shut the postern, the lights sank to rest,
> And into the midnight we galloped abreast.

At the last word Charlie guffawed, until Miss Liers's sharp glance silenced him. "Good, Norah!" she said in a surprised tone, as if her admiration had got in the way of her resentment. "I wish the rest of you could read with such expression."

The rest of them, of course, looked sulky and some of them scowled at Norah. When Dulcie read the next verse in a halting monotone and Miss Liers corrected her, the class smiled in friendly sympathy.

"How was it?" Aunt Mary asked her anxiously, when Norah came out at lunchtime. "Is it very different from your old school?"

"It's bigger," was all Norah replied.

Hanny served her lunch all alone at the polished table. Aunt Mary had to go to a Red Cross meeting.

"Oh, Norah," she said on her way out. "Someone phoned to tell us you are allowed to send home a free cable each month — but you have to select from pre-written messages. The man read them out to me and the most suitable seemed to be 'Now in school and liking it.' Mother agreed that they would send that message to your parents for this month from you and Gavin – isn't that nice? It will get there before any letters. Can you find your way back to school by yourself?" When Norah nodded, she hurried out the door.

Aunt Florence didn't notice her leave for school again; she was upstairs feeding Gavin. "The doctor's been and it's a bad cold," said Hanny. "He's to stay in bed for a week, poor child."

Norah thought he was lucky. And she was glad she didn't have Gavin to worry about at school — taking care of herself was going to be difficult enough.

XIII

Misery Upon Misery

For the rest of the week Dulcie became more and more popular and Norah grew more and more aloof. She pretended she didn't care if no one spoke to her and assumed a cold, proud expression if anyone tried. Ernestine abandoned her. "What a snob," Norah heard her whisper to the others.

It was a relief not to have to go to school on the weekend, but Norah had a hard time finding something to do. Gavin was still in bed, cosseted with tempting food, new toys and Aunt Florence's undivided attention. Aunt Mary seemed to be on a lot of committees.

At least there was Hanny. Norah spent most of Saturday in the kitchen, helping her cook. Hanny asked a lot of questions about England. She was very interested when Norah told her about rationing.

"Two ounces of tea a *week*? However did your

mother manage? Why, sometimes I drink three pots a day! What did you do if you ran out?"

"We never did," said Norah with surprise. "I suppose Mum was just careful." For the first time she realized how difficult it must have been. "Sometimes we were short of sugar and once Dad put one of my acid drops in his tea — because sweets aren't rationed yet. He said it tasted horrible."

"Let's just hope we don't get rationing in Canada," said Hanny, creaming butter and sugar together.

When she'd finished, Norah picked up the eggbeater and licked it. She tried to think of something to ask so they could stop talking about home. "Why hasn't Aunt Mary got a husband?"

Hanny sighed. "Poor Mary. Stifled all her life, then the one chance she had . . ." She pressed her lips closed.

"What?" prompted Norah.

"It's not for young ears. Let's just say she has a secret sorrow." She wouldn't say any more about it.

A Secret Sorrow; it sounded like one of Muriel's romances. Dull Aunt Mary suddenly seemed more interesting.

The cake was put into the oven and Hanny made a pot of tea. "May I have some?" Norah asked hopefully.

"Do you like tea? Sure, I don't see why not." She handed Norah a cup of half-milk, half-tea.

Norah curved her fingers around it and sipped. "*Thank* you!" Hanny smiled at her.

"What about *Mr* Ogilvie?" Norah asked. "What was he like?"

"Ah, what a sad loss to this house when he went. A real gentleman, he was — I don't mean uppity, but a *gentle man*, always kind and thoughtful. He didn't speak much but when he did he said things you wanted to remember. Mary was his favourite — she was absolutely stricken when he died. And so was *she*, of course."

They both knew who "she" was. Norah couldn't imagine Aunt Florence married to a gentle, quiet man.

"She shut herself up for weeks," continued Hanny. "I felt sorry for her, I must admit. First her son, then her husband — the two people she loved best. But that was fifteen years ago and she's long since recovered. She's a strong woman, Mrs O is — too strong for her own good. She was softer when Mr O and Hughie were alive. She needs someone to think about besides herself. Maybe having you two here will use up some of her energy."

Norah shuddered — she didn't *want* Aunt Florence to think about her. "What about you?" she asked, to change the subject. "Did your husband die too?"

"Not him," laughed Hanny. "He's a retired CPR brakeman. Spends his time making model railways now — one day I'll take you and Gavin home to see them. But goodness me, look at the time and I haven't even started the vegetables! You better go and join them in the den — they'll be wondering where you are."

Norah put down her cup and slowly walked out of the comfortable, fragrant kitchen.

Hanny didn't come in until eleven on Sundays, so Norah couldn't escape to her. Instead she had to go to church with the Ogilvies. At least it passed the time. The service was almost the same as at home, with the Smiths sitting in the front pew as usual. Norah found out why Aunt Florence and Aunt Mary turned off the radio whenever she was near: Reverend Milne talked about the terrible bombing London was experiencing. "It's all right, Norah," whispered Aunt Mary, exchanging a worried look with her mother. "I'm sure the bombs weren't anywhere near where your family lives."

Norah's throat felt so constricted that she had a hard time swallowing the huge Sunday lunch. Another dreary afternoon stretched ahead of her and once again she took refuge in the kitchen.

Aunt Florence came in to get some milk for Gavin. "You're in here far too much, Norah," she scolded. "Hanny has work to do — you're getting in her way. And is that tea you're drinking? I'm surprised at you, Hanny — she's much too young for tea."

Hanny pretended not to hear the last part of her sentence. "She doesn't bother me at all, Mrs Ogilvie," she said calmly. "In fact, she's a great help."

"Norah isn't here to be a servant. What would her parents think if we had her doing housework? I want you to stay out of the kitchen, Norah — except for Sunday supper, of course."

Norah opened her mouth to protest, but Aunt Florence silenced her. "No arguments, please. Can't you find anything to do? What about all the puzzles Mary put in your room? Have you done your homework?"

"We didn't have any," said Norah sullenly. "And I've *done* all the puzzles." If she was only to be allowed to talk to Hanny once a week, what *would* she do?

"I know," said Aunt Florence briskly, as she whipped an egg into the glass of milk. "It's time you wrote home. You can do that *every* Sunday afternoon," she added, looking relieved to have thought of a way to occupy Norah.

She settled her in the room behind the den with a pile of thick white monogrammed paper. Norah knelt on the chair drawn up to the oak desk, chewing the end of her pen. She had already written once from the university, but that was just a short note to tell them they'd arrived safely. Now she didn't know what to say. Mr Ogilvie watched sympathetically from his gold frame.

She longed to pour out the truth, to relieve her misery with a litany of complaints. How she had to ask permission every time she left the house and was allowed to explore only within a four-block area. Being forbidden to go into the ravine — although she went there almost every day on her way home from school. Being scolded for biting her nails, for climbing the tree in the front yard and, yesterday, for trying to slide down the laundry chute that led from the second floor to the basement. And school — her isolation and loneliness and the continued resentment of Miss Liers. Just to be able to tell them all this would be a huge relief.

But she couldn't. It would only worry them, when they had the war to worry about. And she knew how disappointed Dad would be if she complained. Grandad would understand, but if she wrote to him separately her parents would wonder why.

Finally Norah thought of a way to fill up the page. She dipped her pen in the crystal bottle of ink and began.

> Dear Mum, Dad and Grandad,
> Here is what is different about Canada. The cars drive on the wrong side of the street. The robins are huge. There is no rationing of food or petrol. There's no black-out. Canadians have different money and they speak a different language. Here is a list of the words I know so far.
>
> Biscuit _____ Cookie
> Sweet _____ Candy
> Lollipop _____ Sucker
> Wireless _____ Radio
> Shop _____ Store
> Flannel _____ Washcloth
> Jersey _____ Sweater
> Lav _____ Washroom
> Headmaster _____ Principal
>
> Dinner is called lunch and tea is dinner. We only have tea on Sundays but we aren't allowed to drink it. Could you tell Aunt Florence that we can?

Did the bombs come near Ringden? Are
there still dogfights? Did any more planes get
shot down? Did Mr Whitlaw's mare have her
foal? Did the hedgehog come back? Have you
heard from Muriel and Tibby? Please answer
soon.

By the end of the letter she was limp with homesickness. Her hand shook as she wrote "Love and kiss-
es from Norah" and added a postscript: "I am cleaning
my teeth every night."

At least writing the letter had taken a good long
time, especially the list. She'd drawn careful straight
lines with the edge of a paper-knife and hadn't made
any blots.

"When do you suppose I'll get a letter from
England?" Norah asked Aunt Florence, going to her in
the den for stamps.

"Not for a while, I'm afraid—the war has made the
overseas mail very slow." Aunt Florence took Norah's
letter and frowned, as if she were displeased it was
sealed. "I hope you didn't mention Gavin's cold, Norah
—we don't want to worry your parents unnecessarily."

"I didn't." Guiltily, Norah realized she hadn't
mentioned Gavin at all.

"I've written as well," said Aunt Florence, holding
up an envelope. "I've told your parents all about our family and sent them a photograph of the house. I'm sure
that will reassure them. I'll get Gavin to draw a nice picture to enclose."

Norah was sure that *her* letter talked about Gavin.

She looked just as curiously at Aunt Florence's envelope as Aunt Florence had looked at hers, wondering what had been said about herself.

On Monday, Norah woke before dawn — something was wrong. "Oh, Gavin — not again!" she groaned, half-asleep. Her bed was cold and wet, as it had been on the boat.

Then she was fully awake and remembered that Gavin wasn't in her bed or even in the room — he was asleep on the floor below. Who had wet the bed?

When she realized, Norah hopped out as quickly as if the bed were on fire. She tore off her wet pyjama bottoms, balled them up and hurled them on the floor.

What was the matter with her? She was ten years old, not a baby! Maybe she was sick. Even so, she didn't want anyone to know what she'd done.

At least no one was up here to see. She took her sheet and pyjama bottoms into the bathroom and rinsed them. She hung them in the wardrobe and closed the door. Then she scrubbed the mattress and made the bed without a bottom sheet. With luck, it would all be dry by evening.

Everything was still damp that night, but Norah put the sheet back on the bed and curled around the wet patch in her other pyjamas. "*Please* don't let it happen again," she prayed. But it did. And the next day after school, Aunt Mary called her into her room.

Norah looked around for evidence of the Secret Sorrow, trying to distract herself from what she guessed Aunt Mary was about to discuss. As in the rest of the house, the room was muffled with dark furniture and curtains. A large Bible lay on the table beside the bed. On the chest of drawers was a photograph of a little girl in a white dress and black stockings, gazing up with adoring eyes to a stalwart-looking boy in a sailor suit. He had one arm circled protectively around her. The boy was handsome, with a thick crop of hair, while the girl was plain and plump. It must be Aunt Mary and her older brother Hugh.

"Sit down, Norah," began the soft voice. "When Edith was doing your room this morning she found a wet sheet and pyjamas hanging in the wardrobe. Did you — did you have an accident?"

Norah nodded unable to speak.

"Do you do this often?"

"Never! I never have before now. Perhaps I'm ill."

"I suppose you're just adjusting. They told us to expect this, but I thought it might happen with Gavin, not a child your age. You'll probably stop eventually." Aunt Mary sighed. "Edith will put a rubber sheet on your mattress. If it keeps on happening, please don't hang your sheets upstairs — put them down the laundry chute. If you leave your bed stripped, Edith will make it up again. And Norah . . . perhaps we won't say anything about this to Mother."

Both their faces were red when Norah left the room. At least Aunt Florence didn't know. It would be a point on her side if she did.

Norah almost became used to scuttling down the stairs with her wet bundle before breakfast each morning. She was relieved Aunt Florence was never up at that time. Edith began to give her resentful looks and mumbled about extra work. Aunt Mary seemed resigned that bed-wetting was part of having war guests, and Norah felt more and more lost and ashamed.

School, too, grew worse instead of better. Miss Liers never praised Norah again; in fact, she seemed to take pleasure in criticizing both her and Dulcie. "Surely it isn't necessary to crowd your words like this," she said coldly, handing back their first compositions. They weren't brave enough to explain that, in England, they'd been encouraged to fill every corner of the page to save paper.

Norah spent recesses standing alone in the corner that was neutral territory between the girls' and boys' playgrounds. She was tired of acting like a princess. She wouldn't mind having a friend, but making friends had always just happened; she didn't know how to be deliberate about it. And by now, everyone had her labelled as stuck-up anyhow.

There was another loner in the schoolyard: a pale boy with glasses and mousy hair that stuck out all over his head like a mop. As Norah watched how the other boys plagued him, she was thankful that at least the girls didn't do things to her; they just ignored her. She wondered why they picked on that particular boy so much.

On Thursday she was just leaving after school when she heard a rhythmic banging come from the middle of a crowd of grade five and six boys.

"*Sauer*kraut, *sauer*kraut," the group chanted. Norah moved closer; she'd heard them call the boy that before.

The boy with glasses was sitting in the dirt in the middle of the group, a bucket inverted on his head. Two boys held him down, while Charlie beat on the iron bucket with a stick in time to the chant.

Norah pushed through the crowd before she had time to think. "Stop that! You're hurting him!"

The group turned with surprise at the sight of a girl interfering. Their victim saw his chance; he pushed off the bucket and fled.

"Why did you *do* that?" Norah asked angrily. She clenched her fists, but her chest constricted at the unfriendly glares of the others.

"Because he's an enemy alien, stupid," said Charlie.

Norah was confused. What did he mean? She didn't have time to ponder, as the group began to close in on her.

Charlie was obviously the ringleader. He was bigger than any of them, and his bright red hair commanded attention like a flag. "You think you're really something, don't you, Limey?" he jeered. "Do you know what *we* think? We think you're a coward. You couldn't take the war, so you ran away to Canada. *We* wouldn't have let them send us away. We'd *like* to be in the war, wouldn't we?" The other boys nodded and waited.

Norah spluttered with fury. "Why — you — you're just a bunch of — of *colonials!*" she finally spat. "I'm *not* a coward! I didn't have any choice about coming here.

And I saw a lot of things you'll never see. I saw a crashed Nazi plane!"

A few of the boys looked interested, but Charlie jeered again. "Naaah, you couldn't have. Enemy planes wouldn't come down that close." He sounded so authoritative that the others looked threatening again.

"They did too!" cried Norah. "They were all around us! And I helped watch for them. What do *you* do? You're the cowards, safe from the war. You wouldn't even know there *was* a war here!"

But they were already moving away. Norah couldn't stop shaking. How was she going to survive this school? The girls ignored her and now the boys despised her. She stopped in the ravine on the way home, first letting herself cry, then thinking for a long time.

She got home late, but no one noticed her sneak upstairs. All of Gavin's belongings, including the rocking horse, had disappeared. Suddenly Norah felt concern. Was Gavin seriously ill? He'd been out of school for almost two weeks, too long for a cold. With shame, she thought of how she'd hardly seen him all that time. Had they taken him to a hospital? She dashed downstairs and into the room where he'd been sleeping.

Gavin was stretched out on the rug, surrounded by a troop of toy soldiers. He was dressed in a navy-blue sailor suit and shiny new shoes.

"Are you still sick?" Norah demanded.

Gavin shook his head. "No, but I'm going to stay in this room all the time now, because I'm delicate. See my new soldiers, Norah? Aunt Florence took me to an enormous shop today called a department store. There was a lift — 'cept it's called an elevator — and six floors. She bought me all sorts of clothes and things and these wizard soldiers. Tomorrow we're going to the museum to see the dinosaurs!"

"Don't be ridiculous, Gavin. If you're better, you'll go to school tomorrow. And you're *not* delicate — you hardly ever get sick."

"He most certainly is." Aunt Florence stood in the doorway, beaming at Gavin. "Don't lie on the floor, sweetness, you'll catch cold again. Norah, there's something I wanted to discuss with you." She hesitated strangely. "I have decided not to send Gavin to school this term. He's been through a great ordeal, coming all the way over here. That large school would be too much for him. I'll build up his strength until Christmas and then we'll see. Perhaps your parents would let me pay for a private school. We'll go on educational outings and I'll read to him every day. He won't be missing anything — they can't do much in school at his age. If he's not going to be six until November, nobody is going to object if he waits until January to start. I've told your parents that it's not customary in Canada to send five-year-olds to school. I know we sent that cable, but my letter will reach them soon." She spoke as if all her arguments had been prepared beforehand; her imperious grey eyes dared Norah to contradict her.

Norah sat down and picked up a lead soldier while she digested this news. It was wrong, of course. It was bad for Gavin to be so pampered, and he would forget everything he had learned last year. Her parents would be upset if they knew that Gavin really could go to school at five. Aunt Florence had lied to them!

She could threaten to write to her parents; Aunt Florence knew she could. The longer she waited for Norah to speak, the more uneasy she looked.

But it would be much handier for Norah if Gavin was kept out of school and out of her care. Because now she had a plan.

Finally she shrugged wearily. "Lucky you, Gavin — school's *awful*."

Aunt Florence didn't seem to have heard the second part of her sentence. "That's settled, then," she said cheerfully. "And *you're* lucky, Norah, to have that big room all to yourself."

Norah couldn't disagree about that. She trudged back up to the tower that was now her own little kingdom and stared out the window at the darkening sky.

XIV

Bernard

Norah woke up early and peeled off her wet sheet before she had time to think about it. Then she got back on top of the bed and reviewed her plan, listening to the slow clomp of the milkman's horse in the street.

She had decided to play truant. Never before had she done something so risky. In Ringden, where everyone was aware of everyone else's affairs, she would be spotted immediately if she were out of school. But Toronto was a large city; no one would know or care.

She had noticed that when Babs had forgotten to bring a note last week, Miss Liers hadn't insisted on one. "Try to remember next time," was all she had said. Perhaps Norah could get away with pretending she'd been ill.

But what if she didn't? What if she were caught? The worst consequence she could imagine was the Ogilvies and the school being very angry. Maybe she

would even be sent to live with another family. It had
always been upsetting to have her parents or her headmaster angry with her, but she had no warm feelings
towards either the Ogilvies or Prince Edward School.
And being sent to another family couldn't be any worse
than being here; it might even be better.

The black cloud mood descended and she felt
reckless and defiant. She could have a whole day of
freedom, without the aggravation of either the Ogilvies
or school.

"May I take my lunch to school?" she asked at
breakfast, trying to keep the nervousness out of her
voice.

Aunt Mary looked pleased. "That would be a help
today. Mother and Gavin will be at the museum and I
have an Altar Guild meeting. It would give Hanny
more time to do the grocery shopping."

Norah left the house as usual and went straight to
her retreat in the ravine. She still hadn't made a fort, but
she'd pulled logs together to form a kind of chair. She
perched on it jubilantly, stripping the leaves off a twig
and trying to ignore guilty thoughts of her parents.

What would they think if they knew? Well, they
didn't; they were too far away. What if Aunt Florence
knew? The fact that *she* didn't made Norah grin with tri-
umph. The only people she wished could see her now
were Charlie and his gang — then they'd know she
wasn't a coward.

She stayed in the cool glen for a long time,
hugging her knees to her chest. She had only planned
as far as not going to school; how to fill the day in front

of her was a challenge. It might be interesting to explore
Toronto, as long as she avoided the museum. But she
didn't know where that was, anyway. Perhaps she
could go for a ride on a streetcar. Aunt Florence had
begun to give her pocket money — she called it
"allowance" — every week. She could have a streetcar
ride, then go somewhere to eat her lunch. There was
still the afternoon, but by then she might have thought
of something else.

Hiding her school books under a bush, Norah
scrambled out of the ravine. She walked rapidly away
from the Ogilvies', her legs trembling. Someone could
still come out and see her.

When she reached Yonge Street, the busy main
thoroughfare that she wasn't supposed to cross, she
stood and blinked with uncertainty for a few seconds.
Streetcars moved up and down amidst the cars, but she
didn't have the courage to board one yet. She began to
walk.

She was right about being anonymous in a big city.
No one seemed to find it unusual to see a ten-year-old
girl walking along the street on a Friday morning. All
the same, she tried to look purposeful.

After about ten minutes, she reached another
busy street and realized she was in a much more
bustling area. They had come by here on their way
from Hart House. This was like exploring Stumble
Wood with Molly and Tom, only the landmarks were
signs and buildings instead of trees.

It was even easier not to be noticed here. Norah
gazed in store windows and wove in and out among

crowds of women carrying shopping bags. Her ears rang with the screech of cars and the bleat of horns; she marvelled how quiet it was in Rosedale, with all this activity so close.

A red and yellow streetcar clattered along a track in the middle of the road and stopped, its bell dinging. Norah noticed how people walked right out onto the street to board. She followed them as the doors unfolded.

"Do you have a ticket?" asked the driver.

Norah shook her head. "How much is it, please?" He told her, and she counted out the change carefully. Even though Miss Liers had given her and Dulcie a lesson in Canadian money, she still wasn't used to it.

"Pay the ticket-taker," said the driver. Norah moved down towards the middle of the car, where she gave her fare to the ticket-taker. She took a seat on one side of the long, thin car. It rocked from side to side as it rumbled along. When someone glanced at her curiously, Norah tried to look as if she belonged to the woman beside her.

She had boarded at Charles Street. After she'd travelled about ten blocks, she got off the streetcar and ran across the road to catch a car going back. Anxiously she peered out at the imposing brick and stone buildings, each one jammed with windows. What a lot of people must be inside! She reached the sign saying Charles Street again, and got off for good.

Exhilarated by her success, Norah almost skipped as she made her way back to Yonge and Bloor. She'd done it! Now Goosey and Loosey weren't the only ones to have ridden on a Toronto streetcar.

As she paused for a red light, she glanced across the street and saw a large woman pulling a small, sailor-suited boy by the hand. Aunt Florence and Gavin! Norah pelted into the doorway of a store and hid.

Aunt Florence stopped to talk to an elegant lady in a flowery hat. She seemed to linger there forever. Norah pretended to be absorbed in a display of women's shoes. Her heart raced as she imagined Aunt Florence's voice cutting through the traffic noise as she shouted, "Norah, *what* are you doing out of school?"

Finally Aunt Florence began walking again, Gavin trotting along behind. He looked unhappy, Norah noticed with surprise — dazed and passive, like a puppy on a lead.

As soon as she thought it was safe, Norah hurried in the other direction. She trudged up Yonge Street with relief. She was getting tired, but she couldn't stop with nowhere to sit. Her stomach gurgled and the soles of her feet stung from the hard pavement. Finally she reached a park. Resting on a bench far away from the street, she ate all the food Hanny had packed for her lunch. A mangy-looking black squirrel and two pigeons shared it with her.

Now what? Norah sighed, wishing she owned a wristwatch. Perhaps she could miss only the morning, but she didn't know when the lunch bell would go. And it was going to be tricky arriving back at the Ogilvies' at her usual time after school. She began to walk again, feeling flat; seeing Aunt Florence had wilted her enthusiasm.

When she reached her own neighbourhood, Norah decided to keep walking north. There was nowhere else to go besides the ravine, and she didn't feel like sitting down there for the rest of the day. By now her legs felt like two lead sticks, but she passed no more parks.

Then she noticed, a few doors down a side street, a sign saying Toronto Public Library — McNair Branch.

Anyone could go into a library. This one was larger than the one in Gilden, but it looked inviting; there was even a sign at a side door saying Boys and Girls.

She pushed open the door timidly and went down the stairs to a long room filled with books and tables. At one end there was a fireplace and a puppet theatre, and at the other a desk with a young woman bent over it. She lifted her head as Norah hesitated by the entrance.

"Good morning!" she greeted. With surprise, Norah saw that the clock on the wall said it was only eleven. "Is there anything I can help you with?" asked the librarian. Her round face smiled eagerly.

"May I look around?" asked Norah shyly.

"Of course! Look around as much as you wish and take any books you want to a table. Are you one of our young war guests?"

How did she know? Norah flushed with confusion until she realized: her accent, of course. "Yes," she said as calmly as possible. "I'm staying with a family in Rosedale but I've been ill, so I don't have to go to school today."

The friendly woman accepted this easily. "My

name is Miss Gleeson. I'm very fond of England, because that's where all my favourite authors are from.
Would you like to apply for a library card? You can take
the form home for your hosts to sign."

"Oh, no — I'll just look at the books here," Norah
said hastily. Then, because Miss Gleeson looked disappointed, she added, "My name's Norah."

"Well, Norah, and what would you like to read?"

"Do you have a book called *Swallowdale*?"

Miss Gleeson shot out of her chair, ran to a row of
green-backed books, snatched one from the shelf and
darted back with it. She held the book aloft as if it were
a sacred object.

"Arthur Ransome! My favourite author! Isn't he
wonderful? Have you read the first one? Have you ever
been to the Lake District? The first thing I'm going to do
after the war is over is to go there and try to find the
places in the books."

Norah wished she could just have the book. She
mumbled an answer and the librarian finally handed
over *Swallowdale*. Norah sat down at one of the tables
and found the place where she'd left off. Miss Gleeson
had returned to her desk, but every time Norah looked
up, the librarian was gazing reverently at her and the
book.

She forgot about Miss Gleeson as the story drew
her into it. For the next two hours Norah scarcely
moved. She was so involved in the escapades of the
Walkers and the Blacketts that she jumped when the
door opened.

"Come in quietly, Bernard," said Miss Gleeson to

the boy who entered. "There's someone reading."

Norah turned over *Swallowdale* and stretched the stiffness out of her arms and legs. She was close to the end and wanted to put off having to finish. She looked at the newcomer more closely; then she quickly held up the book to cover her face.

It was the boy with glasses. She peeked at him over the top of her book, as he went straight to the section marked Other Lands, chose a book and settled with his back to her at the table in front.

Norah studied the washed-out flannel of his plaid shirt. Miss Gleeson had called him Bernard. What was he doing here? Would he recognize her from yesterday and tell someone she wasn't in school? Then it occurred to her that he must be playing truant too; she relaxed and went back to her story.

"Excuse me, children." They both looked up. "I have to go to a meeting. If anyone wants help, could you send them up to the adult department?"

They nodded, and Miss Gleeson left through a door by the fireplace. Norah had finished her book. She closed it with a sigh and sat for a few minutes wondering what to do next. It was only two o'clock; this was the longest day she could remember. She could pick out another Ransome book, but her eyes burned and her head was so full of *Swallowdale* there was no room for a new story.

"Do you mind if I ask why you aren't in school?" The boy had turned around and was looking at her steadily through his round glasses. His eyes were a muddy brown, like the faded colours of his shirt.

Norah could repeat her lie about being ill, but a person her age was much less likely to believe it than a grown-up. And there was something about the boy's freckled face she trusted.

"I'm playing truant," she said. Then, after a pause, she added. "I hate school."

Bernard grinned. "So am I and so do I! You're one of the grade five war guests, aren't you?"

Norah nodded. "And you're in Mr Bartlett's class. I'm Norah Stoakes."

"I'm Bernard . . . Bernard Gunter." He looked sheepish. "Thanks a lot for rescuing me yesterday. I would have come back to thank you then, but I'm not very brave, as you may have noticed." He spoke in a wry, grown-up tone, as if he were older than grade six.

Norah shuddered. "It must have been horrid, all that banging. Charlie's in my class — he's awful!"

"My ears didn't stop ringing until this morning! But I don't care about them. Charlie's such a pea-brain. He's supposed to be in grade seven, but he's flunked twice. How did you get out of going to school today?"

Norah explained how she'd hidden in the ravine and gone for a ride on a streetcar. When Bernard told her he'd convinced his mother he had a stomach-ache that was too painful for school but not painful enough to stay away from the library, they both giggled.

"Why do *you* hate school?" asked Bernard.

It was too complicated to explain. "You first," said Norah.

"Nobody likes me," said Bernard matter of factly. "I guess it's not surprising, with the war on and my last name. We — my mother and I — are beginning to get used to it. Some of the stores in our neighbourhood won't give her credit any more, and sometimes we get anonymous letters telling us to move."

"But what has your last name got to do with it?"

"Gunter is German. Both my parents come from Munich, but I was born in Kitchener. That's where we lived until my father died and we moved to Toronto. My mother thought it would be easier to find work here. She cleans houses for rich ladies."

Norah struggled to take all this in. German! German like Hitler — like the Enemy. She remembered Charlie's words: "an enemy alien".

But Bernard was just an ordinary boy, like Tom. Not really ordinary, though. He'd called himself a coward, but there was something special about him, a kind of dignified inner assurance that wasn't cowardly at all.

"Are you going to not like me too?" asked Bernard calmly, when she didn't reply. "It would be understandable if you didn't, being English. But kind of stupid, I think. I'm a Canadian. I hate Hitler and the Nazis as much as you do. My aunts in Germany don't like them either. We wanted them to come over here, but they're too old to move."

Norah's qualms vanished. If Bernard hated the Nazis, he must be all right. She certainly didn't want to act as stupid as Charlie. And besides, she liked him. Surely that was all that mattered.

She smiled. "I don't care what your last name is." Bernard looked relieved, and Norah suddenly began telling him how she hadn't wanted to come to Canada.

"I can see why you wouldn't want to leave your family," said Bernard. "You're lucky to be able to travel, though. And Canada's a great country — maybe you'll get used to it. What are the people like where you're staying?"

Norah didn't want to talk about them. She shrugged, and Bernard showed her his book about Australia.

"I'm trying to find out about every country in the world. When I grow up, I'm going to visit them all and write articles about them for the *National Geographic*. Mr Bartlett lends them to me. What are *you* going to be?"

"I don't know — I'm only ten!"

"You should decide," said Bernard gravely. "It gives you something to look forward to. When I'm a famous journalist, it won't matter that those guys put a bucket over my head."

Norah listened to him with growing admiration, as he explained more about the countries he'd studied. He knew as much as a teacher. Miss Gleeson smiled at them when she returned; she didn't seem to mind them talking in a library.

Norah noticed the time. "I should go," she whispered. "I have to be home by three-thirty so they won't suspect anything." The two of them exchanged a conspiratorial look and walked out together.

Bernard gave her a ride on the back of his bicycle to her street. "Are you going to school on Monday?" he asked, as if Norah played truant whenever she felt like it.

"I suppose so. Miss Liers might not believe me if

I stay away too long." She remembered something and gulped. "Do you think, if she finds out, I'll get the Strap?" The grade fives were always whispering about the Strap. One day when Charlie had started a fight in the playground, he'd come back from Mr Evans's office with red puffy hands.

"Only boys get the Strap," Bernard assured her. "And I won't, because Mum will give me a note. She knows I have to have a break sometimes. Would you like to come over to my place tomorrow?"

"Sure!" said Norah, trying out some Canadian slang. "I'll have to ask, though."

"Phone me in the morning and let me know." He wrote down his number for her.

Norah skipped down the leafy street, her insides light and airy. Now she remembered how friendship sometimes happened — so quickly that, a little while after you'd met a person, you couldn't believe you hadn't always known each other. Just before she reached the Ogilvies' she remembered to retrieve her books from the ravine.

"May I go over to a friend's house tomorrow?" she asked at dinner.

"How nice, Norah!" smiled Aunt Mary. "I'm glad you've made a friend."

But her mother frowned. "What's her last name?"

"It's a boy — Bernard Gunter."

"Gunter? That's not a name I know. Is this boy in your class?"

"He's in grade six," said Norah. "May I go?" Why did Aunt Florence have to make such a fuss over a simple request?

"I think you'd better have him over here first, then I'll decide. I'm sure your parents wouldn't want you associating with anyone unsuitable."

"They would leave it up to me," blurted out Norah before she could stop herself.

"Enough sauce, my girl! If you'd like to ask this Bernard over for lunch tomorrow, I'll ask Hanny to prepare something special. Then we can all meet him."

Norah finished her dessert in deflated silence. All her elation over having a friend was spoiled. She was sure Bernard would never want to come to the Ogilvies' to be inspected like something from a store brought home on approval.

But to her surprise, he didn't seem to mind. "Mum says they live in a big house," he said on the phone the next morning. "Sometimes she lets me come along to the places she works in — once I found a secret passage! How many rooms are there?"

Norah said she wasn't sure.

"Maybe we can count them," said Bernard. "See you at noon."

She felt better after he had hung up. Lunch was sure to be an ordeal, but it would pass quickly. Then, surely, Norah would be allowed to play with Bernard alone. She decided to show him her shrapnel.

Norah waited on the front steps for Bernard to arrive.

"This place is gigantic!" he exclaimed on the way in. He was very clean and tidy. His unruly hair was somewhat subdued with water, and his blue shirt looked freshly ironed. He was even wearing a tie.

He was also very polite. He said "please" and "thank you" in all the right places and chewed his macaroni in careful small mouthfuls.

"What does your father do, Bernard?" asked Aunt Florence.

Bernard swallowed before he answered. "My father died two years ago. He was a garbage collector."

Aunt Florence gave a small cough as Aunt Mary said gently, "I'm sorry, Bernard. You must miss him."

"Where do you live?" Aunt Florence asked next. "How does your mother manage on her own?" In five minutes she seemed to have found out everything she wanted to know. For the rest of the meal she sat in unusual silence.

Gavin shifted his chair closer and closer to Bernard's. "Do you want to come and see my rocking horse after lunch?" he asked eagerly.

"He wants to look at *my* things," said Norah. "May we please be excused?" Gavin trailed after them, but Norah ignored his wistful look and shut the door of her room before he reached it.

For an hour she and Bernard examined the shrapnel and the old books. Bernard was properly impressed and wanted to know all about the Battle of Britain. He found an old geography book and asked if he could borrow it. "Let's try to count the rooms now," he suggested.

"Not today," said Norah uneasily. "We'd better just stay here." She couldn't decide whether Aunt Florence had approved of Bernard or not. Her silence had been perplexing.

She found out the verdict at dinner. "Your young friend seems very well brought up," said Aunt Florence. "Obviously his mother has absorbed the standards of the homes she works in. But I'm afraid I can't allow you to associate with him, Norah. His background is quite unsuitable — why, his mother works for my friend, Mrs Fitzsimmons! It would just make him uncomfortable to mingle with a family like ours. And then there's his nationality. I don't know why I didn't realize at once that he was German."

"He's Canadian!" cried Norah, throwing down her fork. "And what does it matter what his mother does? At home my friends' parents do all sorts of things!"

"Kindly lower your voice, Norah," commanded Aunt Florence. "A small village is different than a large city — you can't be too careful." Her voice became less harsh. "I'm doing this for your own good. You are part of this family now and it's my duty to take care of you." She sighed. "You should really be going to Brackley Hall, where Mary went."

Norah bristled. "I don't *want* to go to a snooty school! And I'm *not* part of your family! I didn't choose you and I wish I didn't live here!"

There was a shocked silence. Aunt Mary pressed her linen napkin to her lips and Gavin stared at Norah with round, frightened eyes.

Finally Aunt Florence spoke, her voice icy. "Might I remind you that we didn't have a choice either? If we had, I'm sure we would have picked a child who was grateful for the opportunity to live with a privileged family, instead of rude and inconsiderate. We have to put up with *you*, so you had better put up with us. I don't want you to have anything to do with Bernard. That's my decision, and I don't want to hear any more about it."

Aunt Mary took a deep breath. "Mother, isn't that a little hard? He seemed like such a *nice* boy."

"Mary, really! I think Norah had better miss dessert and go straight up to bed." Aunt Florence looked as if she'd like to order her daughter to do the same.

Up in her room Norah tugged on her pyjamas violently, shaking away her angry tears. She glanced at the photograph of her family. Dad's eyes looked reproachful and she remembered his parting words: "If you're impolite or ungrateful, the Canadians will think that's what English children are like." But he'd also said the people she'd be living with would be kind.

She picked up the photograph and shut her parents' faces into her top drawer. Aunt Florence was wrong. Norah couldn't and wouldn't obey her. Bernard would have to be a secret. She would just have to work out a way to see him without Aunt Florence knowing.

Late that night she woke up when she heard a noise on the second floor. It sounded like singing. She crept downstairs and saw a light on in Gavin's room.

Was he ill again? Norah tiptoed along the hall and listened outside his door. It was Aunt Florence who was singing, in a rich, tender voice.

Dance to your daddy,
My bonnie laddie.
Dance to your daddy,
My bonnie lamb.
You shall have a fishie
In a little dishie.
You shall have a fishie
When the boats come home.

"When will I see *my* dad?" asked Gavin. "And my muv . . . . " He sounded as if he had been crying.

"As soon as the war is over, sweetness. But you're with me now, and I'll keep you safe. Is the nightmare all gone now? No more bogeyman? Lie down, then, and I'll sing to you again."

Norah peeked in as the vibrant voice crooned. Aunt Florence was wearing a pink silk dressing gown that made her look soft in the dim light. She was stroking Gavin's hair and her expression was sad and yearning.

"Why are you angry with Norah?" asked Gavin sleepily. "You made her unhappy."

"Your sister has to learn to control her temper," said Aunt Florence stiffly. "But don't worry about Norah, sweetness. She's such a strong girl, I'm sure she's not that upset. Go to sleep, now."

Norah slipped upstairs before Aunt Florence caught her. Gavin didn't *belong* to her, she thought angrily. And what a babyish song for a five-year-old. But she couldn't forget that look of longing. Perhaps Aunt Florence had once sung the song to Hugh.

XV

News from England

Norah stood beside her desk on Monday morning, her chest so heavy she could hardly breathe. Around her, the rest of the class mumbled their way through the Lord's Prayer and "God Save the King." Miss Liers left the piano, returned to her desk and took the roll call.

Why did she have to have a last name so far along the alphabet? Norah sat on her hands to stop them from shaking and Dulcie looked over with surprise. If only Bernard were in her room, someone would understand her agony.

Finally Miss Liers called "Norah Stoakes" in her tight voice.

"Present, Miss Liers."

The teacher raised her head. "You weren't here on Friday, Norah — did you bring a note?"

"I'm — I'm sorry, Miss Liers. At home we didn't need to bring a note when we were sick."

Her voice was so strained, it must have sounded convincing. Miss Liers appeared to believe her. "Here you *do* need one," she said coldly, "but we'll let it go today. Kindly remember next time you are ill." She frowned at the rest of them. "That goes for the whole class. Far too many of you are forgetting."

Norah slouched with relief. It was over, and she'd hardly had to lie. She knew she'd never play truant again. It was too nerve-racking. But now school would not be quite so bad, not when she had a friend to meet at recess.

She found Bernard at the flagpole, as they'd planned. They both looked around warily for Charlie, but he was at the other end of the schoolyard playing football.

Norah didn't know how to tell Bernard he couldn't come to the house again. "Aunt Florence says we're not allowed to see each other," she blurted out awkwardly.

"My mother *said* she might not approve of me. That's why she made me get all dressed up." Bernard's voice was nonchalant, but his eyes looked hurt. "Does this mean we can only meet at school?"

Norah shook her head, grinning. "I've thought of a place we can meet every day, and no one will ever know — the library!"

She got a form from Miss Gleeson that afternoon and took it home for Aunt Florence to sign. From then on, she was allowed to go to the library every day after school. It was a perfect solution, because it was almost legitimate. Norah *did* choose books every day and brought them home. Miss Gleeson had a knack of knowing exactly what she would like and saved new ones for her. When Norah got home she went straight to her room and read until she had to join the Ogilvies in the den before dinner. She often read long into the night as well. No one ever checked on her after she'd been sent upstairs. In school she became sleepy and in- attentive, but the work was easy enough that she didn't fall behind.

Aunt Florence seemed pleased that Norah had found an activity that kept her occupied and out of the way. Norah even heard her boast about it to one of the Sunday evening bridge players: "Norah's turned into a real bookworm," she said, with surprising pride.

But Aunt Mary began watching her anxiously. "You're looking peaky, Norah. I think you spend too much time alone."

What she didn't know, of course, was that Norah wasn't alone. She now took her lunch to school every day; after she gulped it down in the classroom, she and Bernard had half an hour to talk in the playground. It never took her long after school to choose her books. Then they had a whole hour to play.

Often they went to the ravine, descending into it well before they reached the Ogilvies', to be out of sight. They were building a fort under the bridge and carried down old scraps of lumber and cardboard. Bernard had invented a complicated method of making a roof by weaving thin branches together. It took a long time because the branches kept snapping.

The trees were changing colour rapidly and the air

Sandy School Library
Sandy, OR 97055

was as tart as new apples. Horse chestnuts littered the ground in their split green cases. They collected them to make conkers — Bernard called them bullies. At Bernard's place, they baked them hard in the oven, bore holes through them with Mrs Gunter's meat skewer and threaded Bernard's skate laces through the holes.

But their beautifully tough conkers were wasted as they stood on the sidelines of the bully matches that now happened daily in the schoolyard. No one invited Norah and Bernard to compete. Instead, they had to be content with swinging at each other's.

Charlie and his gang seemed reluctant to beat up a girl, so Norah's presence protected Bernard. The boys still shouted "Hun" and "Limey" after them, but they ran away together and tried to laugh.

Bernard lived in one quarter of a "fourplex" on the other side of Yonge Street. "My mum cleans the building, so the rent is cheap," he explained. Sometimes Mrs Gunter was finished work by the time school was out. Then she would greet them with cupcakes and cocoa. She was a large woman who sighed a lot. Her doughy face was always creased with a tired smile, but somehow it still looked sad. "I'm so glad Bernard has a friend," she said the first time Norah met her. Norah hoped he hadn't told his mother that their friendship was forbidden; she didn't want to add to her sadness.

Norah told Mrs Gunter all about her family and her journey to Canada. Even though she was tired of telling the story to the Ogilvies' friends, she didn't mind repeating it to this comfortable woman.

"It's not right that children should have to go through so much," sighed Bernard's mother. "What trying times these are for us all. And your little brother, how is he liking Canada?"

Norah shrugged. "All right, I suppose." It made her uncomfortable to think of Gavin. Yesterday afternoon he had appeared in the doorway of the tower.

"What do *you* want?" Norah had asked, startled from her book. He hadn't been in her room since they had shared it.

"Nothing. I just came up." As if that explained everything, Gavin came in and sat on her bed, swinging his legs.

"*What?*" asked Norah irritably, wanting to get back to her story.

"Norah, do you think Hitler's captured England yet? Will Muv and Dad and Grandad and Joey be prisoners?"

Norah couldn't answer for a second, her throat was so tight. She took a deep breath and tried to sound calm. "No, I don't. We'd hear about it, wouldn't we? And there might not even *be* an invasion."

Suddenly her brother's trusting face made her want to shake him. How was *she* expected to know? He should have asked Aunt Florence.

"Go away now, Gavin, I'm trying to read." She picked up her book and turned her back on him.

But she couldn't read any more. Instead she listened to his slow footsteps descending the stairs and almost called him back.

"Norah?" asked Bernard. "I said, do you want to

go to my room now?"

"Sure!" Norah shut Gavin out of her mind and followed Bernard. As usual they pored over the maps which covered his walls, and then they stretched out on his rug to play Parcheesi and checkers. Norah felt much more at home here than at the Ogilvies'. "Come over as often as you like," urged Mrs Gunter, but she was seldom there herself — she was usually out working.

Escaping into books and having a friend made being a war guest more bearable. But now Norah lay awake worrying about her family. The radio reports from England were worse and worse — London was bombed every night now. She checked the hall table each day for mail, but still no letters came.

On the same Monday she had given her excuse to Miss Liers, Norah heard some shocking news. She was lying on the floor of the den, finishing off the Saturday funny papers. At home, most of the newspaper comics had disappeared because of the paper shortage. "Rupert", her favourite, was still published, but even his adventures had been reduced to one panel at a time. But here there were such thick wads of comics from all the different papers that it often took her several days to get through them. Superman, the Lone Ranger, Tarzan and Flash Gordon — they were all new to Norah and she devoured their adventures with relish.

Aunt Mary was sitting beside Norah reading the *Evening Telegram*. "Oh, *no!*" she gasped.

Aunt Florence jerked up her head. "Gavin, would

you go and fetch my needlepoint?" she said quickly.

As Gavin left the room, Norah jumped up and scanned the front page over Aunt Mary's shoulder. "Children Bound for Toronto Victims of Hitler's Murder," said the bold print.

"What does that mean?" she whispered.

"Let *me* see." Aunt Florence snatched the paper from her daughter. "Disgraceful!" she fumed, when she'd read it. "What I would do to that man if I had a chance . . . "

"*Please,*" choked Norah. "What happened?"

Aunt Florence and Aunt Mary held a kind of silent conversation with their eyes. "I suppose we can tell you, since you're safely over here," said Aunt Florence, "but when Gavin comes back we must stop talking about it. What's happened is that a ship was torpedoed by the Nazis. It was full of evacuees on their way to Canada and many of them were drowned."

"How many?"

Aunt Florence seemed reluctant to answer. "Eighty-seven children and two hundred and six adults," she said finally, her voice unusually thin.

Aunt Mary touched Norah's shoulder. "Thank God it wasn't *your* ship!"

Norah was stunned. All those days at sea she had looked for periscopes she'd never really *believed* the Germans would attack their ship. She remembered Jamie saying he wished they'd be torpedoed. He hadn't believed they would either. It had just been a game — but this was real.

Then she remembered Miss Montague-Scott, who

was hoping to come back again on another ship. "Does it give the names?" she asked in a small voice.

Aunt Florence shook her head. "Not yet — I expect the families haven't been notified." She looked at Norah with sudden, unexpected concern. "I don't want you to brood about this, my dear. I'm sure there was no one you know. Let's just be thankful that you and Gavin made it over here safely."

The two women tried to change the subject, but in the next few weeks Norah kept hearing more about it on the news. The ship was called the *City of Benares* and some of the children thought drowned were rescued after spending days in a lifeboat.

In the meantime, she finally got a packet of letters from home. She whisked it off the table and flew up to the tower. Three letters tumbled out, from Mum, Dad and Tibby. "Dear Norah and Gavin," they each began, but she had to read them by herself before she could share them with him.

"What lucky children you are — it looks as if you're living in a mansion!" said Mum. "We've shown the picture of the house to everyone in the village. Mrs Ogilvie sounds very pleasant — she wrote a reassuring letter. It's too bad Gavin isn't old enough for school but it sounds as if he's having some splendid outings. We feel much better knowing you're both in such a secure home."

Both her parents continued in the same way, expressing relief at their safety, saying how much they missed them and answering some of Norah's questions. "We still see lots of planes and another one crashed near Smarden," said Dad. "It's London that's really getting it now. Everyone is bearing up, though. People are sleeping in the tube. We can sometimes see the reflection of the fires from here. We go into the shelter most nights but don't worry, there's been no damage in Ringden."

Grandad sent his love in a postscript. Tibby told her she and Muriel were being trained as mechanics, which was much more interesting than all the scrubbing and cooking they had been doing. Her letter was spotted with words that had been blacked out, words that looked like place names. "You will probably find that parts of this have been censored," Tibby warned. It was unsettling to think that someone else had already read her words. Muriel had added a note to the bottom of Tibby's letter. "I've met a dreamy lieutenant and we're very much in love." Norah grinned; that was what Muriel always said.

She read the letters again and again, extracting every morsel of news. The only part that made her uncomfortable were some questions for her from Dad: "Norah, we are delighted to know you're learning so much about Canada. Mrs Ogilvie told us all about Gavin, but we'd like to hear more about *you*. Are you happy at the Ogilvies'? Is school all right? Please tell us everything."

But she couldn't. As she wrote home again the following Sunday, Norah still had trouble finding enough to say. She couldn't tell them Gavin was being kept out of school deliberately. She couldn't tell them about Bernard, in case they mentioned him to Aunt Florence. Her letters, too, were censored.

XVI

Gairloch

One Thursday in October, Norah couldn't go to the library to meet Bernard; she had to come straight home from school to help pack. The Ogilvies were driving north for the weekend, to a place called Muskoka.

"You'll like it there Norah," said Aunt Mary eagerly. Her voice was much more animated than usual. "Hugh and I spent all our childhood summers at Gairloch — that's the name of our cottage, and it's on the most beautiful lake in Ontario. Our family has been going there for generations."

Aunt Florence had told Norah she could miss school from Friday to Tuesday. "I'll write you a note — I'm sure your teacher won't mind," she said grandly. "We always go to the cottage for Thanksgiving. It's our last time before next year."

Norah was surprised to learn that Dulcie had been invited to come along. "I thought you'd like someone your own age to explore with," explained Aunt Mary. Dulcie was so busy being popular, Norah hardly spoke to her in school. But when they picked her up early Friday morning, she acted as if nothing had changed.

"Isn't it super to be missing school!" she whispered to Norah. "It was so kind of the Ogilvies to ask me. I hope you don't mind," she added timidly.

Norah shrugged. She was reluctant to admit that it would be a nice change to have someone else to talk to, although she wished it could be Bernard.

Aunt Florence was at the wheel of the long, grey Cadillac. Aunt Mary sat on the other side, with Gavin in the middle; Norah and Dulcie had the whole back seat to themselves — the suitcases and boxes of food were in the trunk. Hanny and Edith were staying behind to look after the house.

The drive took most of the day. The houses in the city became smaller and sparser, then gave way to farms. There were rolling hills and fields dotted with bright orange pumpkins. Norah was astonished at the leaves. In the open country they formed a sea of scarlet and golden hues, wave upon wave glistening against the blue sky. The trees were so radiant, they didn't seem real.

"I do believe the colour this fall is the best we've ever had," said Aunt Florence with satisfaction. She spoke as if she had personally ordered the brilliant display.

For lunch they stopped at the side of the road and had a picnic: chicken and mayonnaise sandwiches on soft white bread, sticks of celery, poppyseed cake and

milk. Everyone, even the two women, took turns going
behind a bush. "You probably think we're being very
primitive," said Aunt Florence, "but it's cleaner than a
gas station." Norah and Dulcie looked at each other and
stifled a giggle at the thought of Aunt Florence squat-
ting in such an undignified position. The farther north
they went, the more the two Ogilvies lost their Toronto stiffness.

After lunch, the fields and hills turned to rock and
trees, broken by sheets of water. When they drove over
a small bridge, Aunt Mary burst into song:

Land of the silver birch
Home of the beaver,
Where still the mighty moose
Wanders at will.
Blue lakes and rocky shore;
We have returned once more.
Boom didi ah dah . . .

She stopped with embarrassment when she noticed the three children staring at her, their mouths
open. "Hugh and I always sang that once we'd crossed
the bridge," she explained sheepishly. "He learned it at
camp. That river was the boundary for Muskoka."

The car plowed northwards. Gavin and Dulcie fell
asleep and Norah's eyelids drooped. But Aunt Florence
didn't tire. She was talking to her daughter about storm
windows and the luck of an Indian summer. What was
an Indian summer? Norah wondered drowsily, looking
out on the empty landscape.

Canada was so big! She had never gone so far in a car. Her parents had never owned one, although Grandad had once fixed up an old Morris. Obviously Aunt Florence liked driving; she stretched her long legs to the pedals and leaned back in the seat as if she were in a comfortable armchair. Norah imagined how it would feel to have the control of such a powerful machine in your hands. Perhaps that's what she would be when she grew up, someone who drove cars.

Finally they pulled into a tiny town that was really just a store, a gas station and a few scattered, shabby houses.

"Everybody out," ordered Aunt Florence. "Now we're going on a boat, Gavin!"

The children woke up again. The little store was beside a vast, ripply lake. Norah breathed in the fresh-smelling air as a man came out of the store and led them to a moored motor launch.

"It's the only way to get there," explained Aunt Mary. "Mr McGuigan always takes us over in his boat. Sometimes we have to make several trips with the food, but it's worth it to be on the island."

Norah whirled around to face her. "Are we going to an *island*?"

"Why yes, Norah, didn't I tell you? It's not a very large one, but it's all ours."

Her expression was as excited as Norah's. An island! Like *Swallows and Amazons* . . .

All the luggage, food and people were loaded into the boat, then it putted across the water. Norah sat at the bow, her hair blowing back and her face showered with cold spray. The water was as clear as green glass; when they slowed down she could see rocks in the depths of it.

In front of them was a hill; on top perched a large circular house with a verandah all around it. "There's the cottage!" beamed Aunt Mary. "There's Gairloch!"

A cottage? It was as big as the Ogilvies' house in Toronto. But it looked friendlier, perhaps because it had a name. They got out onto a wharf and helped carry things up steep steps to the house. Its wooden walls were a faded white and its turreted structure was higgledy-piggledy, as if it had been added on to over the years.

Aunt Florence unlocked the front door. Inside, the cottage was dark because the windows were shuttered. The children helped remove them, and bars of late afternoon sunlight streamed through the space. Unlike the formal Toronto house, the furniture was a colourful conglomeration of mismatched chairs and cushions. An immense stone fireplace filled one wall; the others were patterned in strips of contrasting wood.

"Let me see . . . " mused Aunt Florence. "I think Gavin had better sleep on this floor with Mary and me. You girls take your bags upstairs and you can have your pick of any rooms up there. Mary will make up your beds when you've decided."

There were six enormous bedrooms on the second level. The biggest had two double beds in it. "Would you mind . . . can we both sleep in here?" asked Dulcie. "I'd be frightened sleeping alone."

Norah was worried she'd wet the bed as usual; it

would never do for Dulcie to know about that. But it would also be pleasant to have company for a change; she decided to risk it. "All right. You take that bed and I'll have the one by the window." She threw her suitcase in a corner, impatient to get outside.

They clattered downstairs again. The Ogilvies were unpacking food in a large kitchen with a black wood stove. Both women had changed into faded calico dresses; Aunt Florence's even had a hole in it.

"We'll have supper in about an hour," she told them. "It will take us a while to get the stove going. Why don't you all go out and explore? Be careful of Gavin near the water, Norah — it drops off very quickly."

Norah dashed out the front door, followed by Dulcie and Gavin. She peered through the veil of leaves; all she could see was sky, water and trees. "Come on!" she yelled, catapulting down the hill to the water.

The Ogilvies' grey boathouse had a balcony with an ornate white railing skirting its upper storey. It was as big as Little Whitebull. More fancy boathouses and huge "cottages" dotted the shoreline opposite. The children dipped their hands in the icy water and ventured gingerly onto the diving board that jutted off the wharf.

Then Norah had to run. She led the others up the steps. First they circled the steep shore until they came back to their starting place; it really *was* an island. Then they scrambled up over the rocks until they collapsed on a promontory. The lake was spread below like a wrinkled blue sea. Along the horizon the trees blazed like a fire, here and there broken by dark firs and the white lines of birches.

"I'm tired, Norah," complained Gavin. "You went too fast."

"You're just lazy," laughed Norah. "You've been pampered too much."

Dulcie panted. "I'm tired too. May we rest here a minute? Isn't it gorgeous? You *are* lucky to be able to come here all summer."

"All summer?" repeated Norah. In the summer the water might be warm enough for swimming.

"Aunt Dorothy said the Ogilvies stay here from June to September. Maybe they'll even let you out of school early! The Milnes go to a cottage too, on Georgian Bay, but only for two weeks."

Norah couldn't imagine next summer — would they still be in Canada?

"Children! Suppertime!" Aunt Mary's voice floated up to them.

The meal had been cooked by Aunt Florence herself. There were sausages and baked potatoes and huge McIntosh apples. They ate around the kitchen table. "A very good supper, if I do say so myself," said Aunt Florence. "Don't you think I'm a good cook, Gavin?" Norah looked at her curiously. If Aunt Florence liked her own cooking so much, why did Hanny always do it at home?

Aunt Florence handed Norah a cup of tea. Mum had written to her and given permission for Norah and Gavin to have it.

"Are *you* allowed to drink tea, Dulcie?"

"Oh yes, Mrs Ogilvie. Aunt Dorothy says we can

have whatever we're used to at home."

Aunt Florence sniffed disapprovingly and Norah tried not to grin as she slurped the familiar milky liquid.

"This is a very large cottage, Miss Ogilvie," said Dulcie to Aunt Mary. "Did you used to have more people in your family?"

Aunt Florence answered for her daughter. "It doesn't just belong to us, Dulcie. My father and his brothers built it. Their name was Drummond, which was mine too, of course. All the Drummonds share Gairloch. In the old days they travelled up by train and steamer and brought lots of servants. Hanny and her husband come with us in the summers, but we always rough it in October."

"There are so many relatives that some of them stay in cabins down the hill," said Aunt Mary. "The older children either sleep in the old servants' quarters in the back or on top of the boathouse. We call them the Boys' Dorm and the Girls' Dorm. You'll be over the boathouse, Norah — there are several girl cousins your age."

Norah digested this. "Why aren't they here now?" she asked, although she was glad they weren't. It was far better to have Gairloch to herself.

"Most of our family lives in Montreal," explained Aunt Mary. "It's too far for them to come for just the weekend, but you'll meet some of them at Christmas."

"Mary and I stay in the main cottage, of course," said Aunt Florence. "I am the oldest living Drummond, so I'm the head of the clan, so to speak." She puffed herself up like a peacock.

Norah felt herself grow proud too. Even though she was only a war guest, if Aunt Florence was the head of the family her reflected glory would surely give Norah some status among all those cousins next summer. If she were still here next summer, of course.

"It's almost time for little boys to be in bed," said Aunt Florence fondly. "Norah, you help Gavin find his pyjamas and you and Dulcie get ready yourselves. We'll tackle the dishes."

After she was in her pyjamas and dressing gown, Norah wandered onto the verandah and sat down on a seat that swung from chains. The night was as black, and the stars shone as brightly, as at home. She searched the sky for the Great Bear, surprised to find it looking exactly the same. Could *they* see it while she saw it? she wondered. The air was brisker than in the city: her breath clouded in front of her.

"Norah, come in — you'll catch cold!" called Aunt Mary. Norah stayed a few more minutes to chill her skin thoroughly, then ran in to enjoy it tingle in front of the roaring fire.

"Now I will read aloud," announced Aunt Florence. "We always do at the cottage." She picked out a worn, leather-covered book from a low bookcase. "This is called *The Jungle Book*. You should enjoy it, Gavin, it was Hugh's favourite." She opened the book, made sure everyone was attentive, and began. " 'It was seven o'clock of a very warm evening in the Seeonee hills when Father Wolf woke up from his day's rest, scratched himself, yawned, and spread out his paws one after the other to get rid of the sleepy feeling in the tips.' "

Gavin soon fell asleep, leaning against Aunt Florence, but the story kept Norah awake. Aunt Florence was a wonderful reader. Her resonant voice made the story of the wolves and Mowgli come to life. Sitting here like this was so much nicer than after dinner in the city, being bored while the Ogilvies read the paper, played cards or listened to the radio.

Aunt Florence closed the book and Norah and Dulcie stumbled upstairs. They both fell asleep instantly.

To her relief, Norah woke up in a dry bed. The morning was gloriously sunny, with a hint of wind. After breakfast Gavin played contentedly with his soldiers in the dirt under the verandah. Norah and Dulcie tried fishing with some old poles they found in the boathouse. Norah dug up some worms, but Dulcie made so much fuss about putting them on the hooks, they had to stop. They climbed as high as they could go onto the rocks, then went down the hill and peeked into the windows of the locked family cabins.

In the afternoon Aunt Mary took them out in the rowboat. It had velvet cushions and three sets of oarlocks. Each of them tried rowing and Aunt Mary surprised Norah by being very good at it. Her face seemed serene and somehow young. "In the summer we use the motor launch and go on picnics to some of those other islands," she said, pointing them out. "All the children know how to run the motor — you'll learn quickly, Norah." Every time next summer was mentioned, Norah wondered anew about this unexpected future she hadn't thought about.

That evening a few neighbours, also here to close up their cottages, arrived in their boats. They all asked Norah and Dulcie how they liked Canada.

"Isn't it tiring how they always do?" whispered Dulcie at supper. "I always just say 'fine.'" Norah nodded, pleased that Dulcie felt the same way. Dulcie really wasn't a bad sort — if only she were braver.

After the guests had left, they went to bed late; but Norah and Dulcie weren't tired. They lay awake and talked about school.

"I wish Miss Liers liked us better," sighed Dulcie. "I can't do anything right for her."

"She hates Charlie even more than us," said Norah. "I thought she was going to hit him with the pointer when he was so rude last week."

"I wish she had! I'm scared of Charlie. He pulls Ernestine's hair and he calls me 'Limey.'"

"He does?" Norah thought she was the only one in their class he taunted.

"Even so, I like this school better than the one in Ringden," continued Dulcie. "The work's far easier and nobody calls me Goosey here. Babs and Ernestine are ever so nice. I go over to their houses almost every day and we dress up and pretend we're movie stars."

If that was what they did, Norah was glad they didn't like her.

"I know this isn't my business, Norah," said Dulcie slowly, "but everyone notices that you're friends with Bernard Gunter. Girls don't play with boys here.

They would like you better if you didn't. And you shouldn't associate with someone who's German. What if he's a spy?"

"He's not! He's a *Canadian*, not a German. And I can be friends with whoever I choose!"

"Of course," said Dulcie quickly. She prattled on, changing the subject. "Mrs Ogilvie really isn't that bad. And *Miss* Ogilvie is kind."

"She's all right, I suppose. But Aunt Florence is a bossy snob. She may seem nice here, but in the city she's horrid! I'll never like her."

"Oh." There was a long, awkward silence.

"Have you had many letters from Ringden?" asked Norah. And suddenly their words tumbled over each other's as they told what they'd heard from home. Norah had almost forgotten that Dulcie came from the same place.

Finally they finished talking about everybody in the village. "Do you know what, Norah?" Dulcie asked, sounding drowsy.

"What?" Norah lay on her back and stared at the moon through the trees.

"Sometimes I forget what Mummy and Daddy look like. I try and try, but I can't imagine their faces. And it hasn't even been two months since I've seen them. What if we stay in Canada for a year? I might not know them at all!" Dulcie's voice was small and scared. "Do you remember what your parents look like? And your sisters and grandfather?"

Norah said loudly, "Of course I do! Anyway, I have a picture of them. Don't you?"

"No, but that's a good idea. I'll ask Mummy to send one." Dulcie sounded more cheerful. Her voice stopped and her breathing became regular.

Norah sat up in bed to lighten the weight on her chest. She tried to picture her mother's face. Thin blonde hair and blue eyes — or were they grey? Panicking, she tried her father. The different parts of his face came clear — his dark hair streaked with grey and his long, beakish nose — but she couldn't make them fit together.

She did have the photograph, but it was a few years old. Norah fell asleep trying to conjure up the images of her sisters.

The weather was clear for the next two days, too sunny to dwell on thoughts of home. They spent the time in blissful, wandering freedom. Aunt Florence said that, as long as they wore life jackets, the three of them could take out the rowboat alone. They went for long, slow rides around the island; the boat was so heavy, it was a struggle to move it at all. There was a near disaster when Creature fell overboard, but Norah scooped him out before he sank.

At noon on Monday they all gathered around an ancient radio to listen to a message from Princess Elizabeth to the evacuated British children. "My sister Margaret Rose and I feel so much for you, as we know from experience what it means to be away from those we love most of all . . . " said the clipped voice.

Norah listened intently as Margaret Rose obeyed her sister's instructions to say good-night. It was the first time she'd ever heard her voice. She wondered where *they* were spending the war. A month ago, Buckingham Palace had been bombed. Would Princess Margaret Rose feel glad to have been safely away from it, or would she wish she'd been there for the excitement?

"Isn't that touching?" said Aunt Mary when the message was over. "That must be a comfort to you, girls."

Norah and Dulcie glanced at each other self-consciously. It felt both embarrassing and important to have a radio broadcast directed especially to them.

That night more neighbours came in to help celebrate Canadian Thanksgiving. They ate turkey, mashed potatoes and pumpkin pie, a new kind of food. Dulcie whispered that it wasn't sweet enough and only touched the whipped cream, but Norah liked its raw, rooty taste.

Aunt Mary looked sad as Norah helped her close the shutters early Tuesday morning. "Gairloch always looks so desolate when it's shut up like this. I hate to think of how long it will be until we come again."

"When will that be?"

"The Victoria Day weekend in May. That's when everyone opens up their cottages. There are fireworks and a big bonfire at the Kirkpatricks'." She smiled. "I'm glad you and Gavin will be sharing that with us. And in June we'll have three whole months! Just wait until you try the water — it's so clean, you hardly have to wash your hair all summer."

"But will we still be in Canada then? Dad said we'd stay for *perhaps* a year."

"Oh, Norah . . . did you think it was only for a year?" Aunt Mary looked apologetic. "It could easily be for years, now. It looks as if this war will go on longer than any of us expected. Do you mind very much? It's so hard for you, I know, but you already feel like part of the family. And every summer we'll be at Gairloch. You do like it here, don't you?"

"Yes. I like it *here,*" said Norah angrily. She ran away before Aunt Mary could say more. Sullenly she helped load the boat. All the way back to Toronto she ignored Dulcie's hurt look as she refused to talk the way they had earlier.

"For years." That was an eternity. Surely Aunt Mary was wrong. As soon as they got back to Toronto Norah took out her family photograph again, but the faces looked too far away to be real.

XVII

Paige

After Norah's outburst, Aunt Mary began to pay more attention to her, as if Norah were as much her concern as Gavin was Aunt Florence's. Every night she came up to the tower to say good-night, which made Norah feel guilty when she switched on the light later to read. She inquired about Norah's bed-wetting, which had returned, and took her to see a doctor. They told Aunt Florence they were going for a drive.

"That's not really a lie," said Aunt Mary in the car. "We *are* driving, and after the doctor I'll take you along the lake." She tittered nervously; Norah was amazed at her defiance.

"There's nothing physically wrong with her," said Dr Morris, after an examination that made Norah blush all over with shame. "I'm sure it will disappear in time." He advised nothing to drink from dinner until bed-time, and occasionally that worked.

"Mary thinks you should get to know more children your own age," Aunt Florence told Norah one Saturday morning. "I've been meaning to have you meet the children of some family friends, but they've been away, visiting in Massachusetts. Frank Worsley was my son's closest friend; he's the editor of one of Toronto's newspapers. They only live a few blocks from here, and you and Gavin have been invited for lunch today. They have three little girls, aged ten, eight and seven."

Norah had planned to sneak off to a Gene Autry movie with Bernard. "I have something to look up in the library for school," she tried.

"It can wait. Go and change, please. The Worsley girls are always perfectly dressed."

They sounded awful. Sulkily, Norah stood beside Gavin a few minutes later to be inspected.

"I wish you'd let me buy you some clothes, Norah." Aunt Florence sighed at the skimpy Viyella dress that Norah wore every Sunday for church. "Wouldn't you *like* a pretty new dress?"

"No, thank you," said Norah haughtily. She was not going to be beholden to Aunt Florence for more than she had to.

They were allowed to walk by themselves to the Worsleys'. Aunt Florence gave them directions and waved goodbye from the steps. "Remember to say thank you," she called. Norah scowled; did she think their mother hadn't taught them any manners?

She shuffled through the crunchy carpet of leaves on the boulevard. Some drifted down from the tall branches, turning slowly in the sun. "Fall" was a much better word than "autumn", Norah decided. The air was acrid and smoky; it reminded her for some reason of the downed Nazi plane, but then she realized it was only the smell of the heaped, burning leaves in the street. She and Gavin dawdled along the curb, poking sticks into the smouldering piles. A man walked along the other side of the street with a wheelbarrow, calling out "Dry wo-ooo-oood!"

"What's it like at school, Norah?" Gavin asked suddenly.

Norah shrugged. "As boring as school usually is. You're lucky you don't have to go this year."

"I'd like to," said Gavin.

Norah glanced at her brother's wistful face; it was like looking at a stranger. She was almost never alone with Gavin any more. When she got back from playing with Bernard she went straight to her tower and the rest of the time they were with the Ogilvies. Could Gavin be unhappy? Of course he wasn't — he was being given treats and outings every day. "You said you didn't like school," she reminded him.

Gavin looked confused. "That was before. Norah, could you ask . . . "

But they'd reached the Worsleys'. "I know this house!" interrupted Norah.

It was the one where the friendly dog had greeted her on her first walk. What a long time ago that seemed! Now the dog yapped inside as they stood hesitantly on the doorstep. Norah lifted one leg at a time and brushed off the bits of dry leaves that stuck to her socks.

"Aren't you going to knock, Norah?" asked Gavin, but he quickly took her hand when she did.

A very tall, narrow man holding a pipe opened the door. He looked as if he had been squashed vertically; even his hair was tall. "You must be Norah and Gavin," he smiled. The wiry terrier leapt up at each of them, trying to lick their faces. Gavin pushed it away with a whimper.

"Off, Thistle!" the man ordered. The little dog ignored him and continued to bounce up and down as if it were on springs. Norah bent and picked it up; it wriggled in her arms and slobbered all over her face.

"I'm Mr Worsley," said the man. "Aren't you brave to dare to eat lunch with my daughters! From the sounds of things, they might be planning to eat *you*! Follow me and I'll introduce you."

Gavin gripped Norah's hand as they climbed a winding staircase. The inside of the house was as grand as the Ogilvies', but its white walls and pale furniture made it seem airier.

Squeals and shrieks came from an upstairs room. "Peace!" laughed Mr Worsley. "Come and meet your guests. Norah and Gavin, here are my three wild daughters."

Paige, Barbara and Daphne Worsley were in identical tartan dresses, with navy-blue bows tied at the ends of their long blonde braids; they were like three matching dolls in descending sizes. But Daphne had ink smeared on her leg, one of Barbara's ribbons hung in a streamer and Paige's cheeks were daubed with slashes of red paint. Norah's spirits rose — they looked as if their ladylike outfits were disguises.

"Be merciful," admonished their father. "I'm going to pick up your mother from the hairdresser's. Ellen is in the kitchen if you need anything. We'll be back in time for lunch." He left the room.

"Oh good, another *small* person!" The eldest, Paige, pinched Gavin's thigh. "How would you like to be a dinner for cannibals? We've just finished eating Daphne and we're still hungry."

"No, thank you," whispered Gavin, but Paige had already begun to tie him up with a skipping rope.

"Here, I'll help you," said Norah, delighted. "Don't worry, Gavin, it's only a game."

Gavin was trussed and set in the middle of a table, while the cannibals leapt and whooped around it. He smiled uneasily, not sure if he was enjoying this or not. Then they untied him and each chose a part to eat.

"Not as fat as Daphne!" said Barbara.

"I'll take this arm," said Paige, making munching sounds from his wrist to his neck. "Yum, yum!" Gavin looked relieved after all of him had been eaten.

"Let's play cowboys now," suggested Paige. "Norah and I will be the Lone Ranger and Tonto, and Barbara and Daphne will be our horses. Gavin, you and Thistle can be little colts who follow along."

Gavin enjoyed being a colt much more than he had being a cannibals' dinner. They fashioned reins out of dressing-gown belts and drove their horses up and down the stairs and all around the huge house, shooting imaginary guns all the way. Thistle raced circles around them, barking frantically and trying to grab the ends of the reins.

"Whoa!" said Mr Worsley, as he came in the front door with his wife. "Chow time."

At lunch, each Worsley girl competed to say something in a high, shrieking voice. Norah sat beside Mrs Worsley and answered the usual questions.

"I'm sure you'll like it in Canada," she said quietly. She was a glamorous woman, with large green eyes and thick smooth hair like a movie star's. "We're delighted you're living so close. I hope you'll consider our house yours, although you might find my girls overwhelming." She gazed at them with puzzled affection, as if she were not sure they were really hers. They were badgering their father loudly for their allowance.

"Come on, Norah," said Paige, who had already claimed her as her property. "Let's leave the babies and go to my room."

Paige's bedroom was a wonderland of every conceivable toy, game and book that anyone would want. As in Norah's room at home, there was a shelf of pristine dolls and some model planes hanging from the ceiling.

"I have planes like this!" cried Norah.

Paige took out her collection of coloured pictures of British aeroplanes. "They're free — just ask your cook to save your syrup labels, and you can send away for some too."

Norah told Paige about the Skywatchers and the crashed plane. Paige was entranced. "We could start something like that here, except there aren't any enemy planes to watch for. You were *lucky,* being right in the middle of the war." She made Norah feel like a hero and said nothing about anyone being a coward for leaving England.

"What school do you go to?" Paige asked.

"Prince Edward."

"I wish I could go to a public school. Brackley Hall is really strict — I'm always getting into trouble. There's lots of sports, though. I'm very good at basketball because I'm so tall. If only we went to the same school! All the girls in my class are so boring."

Norah thought of Dulcie, Babs and Ernestine. "They are in mine, too."

"I tried to make friends with some of our war guests. A whole school of them came to Brackley with their teachers. But they stick to themselves."

Paige then startled her by climbing onto a stool and hanging upside down by her knees from the door of the wardrobe. The ends of her braids trailed on the floor. "How would *you* like to be friends with me?" she asked casually.

They were so easy together already that it seemed unnecessary to ask. But Norah felt an uncomfortable twinge of betrayal: what about Bernard? He was probably in the library right now, wondering where she was.

"Sure," she answered, just as casually. She paused. "I have one friend at school who's not a bore. He's a boy."

Paige put her hands on the stool and flipped her legs off the door to the rug. "Well, obviously *he* is!" she panted, her face red. She didn't seem to find it unusual to be friends with a boy.

"And he's . . . German," continued Norah. "His parents came from there, anyway. But he's not a Nazi," she added hastily.

"A Nazi! I wouldn't think so. Lots of Germans have come to Canada. Dad has a friend called Mr Braun who works with him at the paper. Sometimes he gets threatening phone calls telling him to leave the country — and he's a Canadian! People are so dumb."

"Aunt Florence — Mrs Ogilvie — doesn't like Bernard. I don't know if it's because of his last name or because his mother's a cleaning lady."

"Probably both! Dad says she's a terrible snob. When he and her son Hugh were young, there were boys he wasn't allowed to see and he had to meet them in this house — Dad grew up here."

"That's just like me!" Norah felt a sudden link with Aunt Mary's brother. "Aunt Florence says I'm not allowed to associate with Bernard. But I do anyway — we meet secretly at the library. Maybe you could meet us there too and we could show you the fort we're building."

"Sure! Or you and Bernard could come here!"

"We couldn't do that — not when your parents know the Ogilvies. They might say something."

"I'll tell you what," said Paige eagerly. "We'll give Bernard another name and pretend he's *my* friend. Then if Mrs Ogilvie ever hears about him she won't know. Bring him over on Monday. I'll show you our secret hideaway in the basement."

Paige was certainly bossy, but she was bossy in such an enthusiastic way that Norah couldn't help being swept up in her plans. She took Norah up to a cavernous attic, where they tried on old clothes from a trunk. Barbara followed them and the three of them played gangsters. Paige and Norah put on slouchy hats and talked out of the sides of their mouths. Barbara wanted to wear one of the elegant dresses and be their girlfriend. "She's sometimes like this," Paige apologized. "It's handy, though, when you need a girl. She's always Maid Marian when we play Robin Hood."

The afternoon sped by so fast, Norah couldn't believe it when Mrs Worsley called up to them that it was time to go. Gavin waited in the hall, holding Mrs Worsley's hand. He looked as if he had been crying blue tears.

"That Daphne . . . " sighed Mrs Worsley. "She tried to dye Gavin's hair — luckily it was washable ink. But I've sent her to her room and we've had a peaceful time playing the piano together, haven't we, Gavin? It's such a nice change to have a quiet little boy in the house. I'm sure I got all the ink out, Norah. Please tell Mrs Ogilvie that I'm very sorry and that I hope she'll let you come again."

When Norah explained why Gavin's hair was wet, Aunt Florence just chuckled. "Frank's children are certainly a handful — just like *he* was as a boy. How did you get along? Would you like to have them all over here sometime?"

"Not Daphne!" whispered Gavin. "I don't like her, and Barbara tried to dress me up like a girl."

"We won't have them if you don't want to, sweet-ness," soothed Aunt Florence. "What about you, Norah? Would you like to invite Paige over? She would be a suitable friend for you."

Norah didn't understand how wild Paige could be more suitable than polite Bernard. But she smiled at Aunt Florence in spite of herself. "That would be nice, thank you."

When Paige and Bernard met on Monday, they took to each other at once. The two were so different that they filled in each other's gaps: Paige's loud and lively nature was balanced by Bernard's thoughtful calm. Norah fit neatly in between, like the filling in a sandwich.

The three of them met almost every day after school and every weekend, sometimes at the library and more often at Paige's. This was easy to arrange be-cause Norah was allowed to go to the Worsleys' whenever she wanted. They called Bernard "Albert", his middle name, and said Paige had met him at the library — which was the truth, of course.

Mr and Mrs Worsley accepted "Albert" as easily as they did everything their daughters did and only inter-rupted their long afternoons of play to suggest snacks. Norah thought Paige's parents were practically perfect. The only conflict Paige had with them was about clothes. Lined up in her wardrobe was a long row of dresses that matched her sisters'.

"When I'm thirteen I won't have to look like Barbara and Daphne any more." She sighed. "That's still so far away. It's such a trial, but it amuses Mother.

You'd think we were the Quints!"

"Who?"

"The Dionne Quintuplets." Now Norah remembered her mother mentioning them.

"We went to see them once," said Paige. "We drove up north and lined up for hours, then we went through a kind of tunnel and watched them through a screen. They were riding around on five tricycles. It was really weird, like looking at animals in a zoo."

"Are they really exactly alike?"

"Exactly. Like five Daphnes — yeech!"

Dressing alike seemed a small price to pay for belonging to such a happy-go-lucky family. If only she and Gavin had been sent *here* to live! Norah spent as much time as she could at the Worsleys'. So did Bernard; he told her he liked going there instead of to the empty house he came home to almost every day.

Paige had come over to the Ogilvies' a few times, but it was hard to think of something to do in their silent house. And they all preferred to play outside, either in the ravine or in the Worsleys' large backyard. Paige thought of a new, elaborate game each week. They played at being Captain Marvel, Knights of the Round Table and all the characters in *The Wizard of Oz*. They tried to train Thistle to be as obedient as Toto, but the stubborn little dog was as rowdy as his owners. At first Norah wondered if Bernard would think he was too old for pretending, but he joined in.

It was Norah who made up the game of Spitfires and Messerschmitts, but both she and Bernard insisted upon being RAF pilots.

"There's no way I'm being a Nazi," said Bernard quietly.

"It's only a game," said Paige. "Okay, *I'll* fly a Messerschmitt — so will Barbara."

It *was* only a game, thought Norah as they roared around machine gunning each other. It didn't really matter which side she was on. But she thought of Tom and proudly piloted her imaginary Spitfire. Then she roared even louder to drown out the painful thoughts of what he and the other Skywatchers would be doing.

Sometimes they went exploring on bicycles, when they could persuade Barbara to lend hers to Norah. It was too small, and her legs became cramped from being bent in the same position. She thought longingly of her own bicycle. Would it be rusted by the time she got back to Ringden?

"If only you had a proper bike, we could go all the way to the beach," complained Paige. "Couldn't you ask for one for Christmas?"

Ask Aunt Florence for something as expensive and important as a bicycle? It was impossible. Norah was sure that Aunt Florence would never approve of her having one anyway, not if she suspected how free it would make Norah. Once the three of them had even ventured downtown, carefully avoiding cars and the treacherous streetcar tracks.

"Come right home from school today, Norah," said Aunt Florence one Thursday. "A social worker is coming to see how you're getting along."

Reluctantly, Norah told Paige by telephone and

Bernard at recess that she couldn't meet them. After school she was made to wash and put on clean white socks. Then she and Gavin were brought into the living room and introduced to Mrs Moore, a merry, round woman in a tight dress that was popping its buttons. Around her were the remains of tea; she must have already spoken to the Ogilvies. Aunt Florence left Norah and Gavin alone with her.

"Well!" she began, a bit too cheerfully. "Aren't you lucky to have come to such a luxurious home! Are you happy living here? Is there anything you'd like to tell me?"

If she had been asked this a few weeks ago, Norah might have unloaded the burden of her misery and homesickness. Now she was filled with confusion.

She only used the Ogilvies' house for sleeping, eating and reading. She still wet the bed almost every night and, most of all, she still wanted to go home. But if she said these things they might send her to another family — then she would lose Bernard and Paige.

"I have a smashing room," she said, trying to be as truthful as possible, "and Hanny is a very good cook. And I've made two friends," she added proudly.

The woman laughed. "Two friends already! Well done! And how are you getting along at school?"

"Fine." She could only lie about that. Even with Bernard as an ally, school was as lonely as ever.

"That's good. And I can tell Gavin is thriving here — look at those rosy cheeks! I'm sure that next year he'll be strong enough for school." Gavin sat quietly, stroking his elephant.

He was *too* quiet, these days, Norah thought uncomfortably. It probably wasn't good for him to spend
so much time following Aunt Florence in and out of
stores. He was often left alone, as well — sometimes
when she came in he was playing by himself in the hall.
She remembered him saying he wanted to go to school.
She could tell Mrs Moore that he should go there now
— and that he always had rosy cheeks. But she remembered again that then she'd have to take care of him. It
would be a waste of her precious after-school time to
have to bring Gavin home every day.

Mrs Moore passed them the cake and nibbled on
a huge piece herself. "The Ogilvies' cook *is* excellent,"
she said. "This is delicious! I think we can assume that
this home was a good match for you two. You seem to
have adjusted very well. Are you looking forward to
our Canadian winter? You'll find our weather much
colder than yours. We have *snow* here — you'll love it!"

"But we have snow," said Norah. "Last winter
there was so much that the roads were blocked and all
the stores were closed. It was so cold that some birds
were frozen to the branches."

"Oh." Mrs Moore looked disappointed. Then she
brightened. "Is there anything at all I can do for you?
Anything you need?"

Could Mrs Moore get her a bicycle? Would she pay
for it, so she wouldn't have to ask Aunt Florence? Norah
knew she wouldn't. She shook her head and said
politely, "No thank you, there's nothing we need."

Mrs Moore spoke privately to the Ogilvies again.
After she left, Aunt Florence looked relieved. "I'm glad

you didn't find anything to complain about, Norah," she said awkwardly.

"You *are* happier, aren't you?" Aunt Mary's face was so pleading that it was for her that Norah answered. "Yes, thank you. May I go over to Paige's now?"

XVIII

The Witches Are Out

Towards the end of October, the last of the leaves blew off the trees and the weather became colder; one morning there was even an icing of snow on the ground. Norah's bare legs tingled when she came in, and she puffed on the tops of her fingers to warm them. Mum had sent the long knitted leggings Norah wore last winter under her skirts, but none of the Canadian girls seemed to wear them, so she left them in her drawer.

Then Aunt Florence took her and Gavin to Simpson's to buy them winter clothes. They picked out two-piece snowsuits, close-fitting hats called toques, wool scarves and mitts, and buckled rubber galoshes lined with fleece. There were knee-length britches for Gavin and, for Norah, itchy wool stockings that were held up by complicated garters.

Aunt Florence wanted to buy Norah a new party dress as well. "You can have your choice of any of these," she said grandly.

Norah looked curiously at the bright dresses hanging in the girls' department. She'd never had a store-bought dress; she usually wore hand-me-downs from her sisters. She thought of how the Viyella dress chafed her armpits. But she'd already accepted enough of Aunt Florence's charity; she could ask her mother to make her a new dress.

"No, thank you."

"You're being very stubborn, you know. I *like* buying you things."

Did she? Or did she just want Norah to look respectable . . . Norah couldn't decide. And she had more important things to think about than clothes: in two days it would be Hallowe'en.

"What's Hallowe'en?" she had asked when Paige and Bernard had gone on about it.

"Don't you *know*?" They interrupted each other in their eagerness to tell Norah about dressing up and going out at night to collect treats from the neighbourhood.

"Isn't there Hallowe'en in England?" asked Bernard.

"I'm not sure — not where I live, anyway. But in November we have Bonfire Night."

"What's that?"

"It's for Guy Fawkes Day. We make a Guy — like a big rag doll — out of old clothes, and we put him in a wagon and take him through the village for a few days, calling 'a penny for the guy.' Then we use the money to buy fireworks. We stuff the Guy with the

fireworks and burn him in a huge bonfire on the green
— everyone dances around it. Except last year we wer-
en't allowed to have one because of the black-out."

They wouldn't be able to this year, either, she
thought sadly. But Hallowe'en sounded just as thrilling.
She joined in the excited plans about costumes.

"We could be Guys!" suggested Paige. "Aren't they
sort of like tramps? All we'd have to do would be to
wear old clothes — you could ask the Ogilvies for some,
Norah."

Norah wondered if she would be allowed to participate in such lawless-sounding activities. Aunt Florence, however, seemed to approve of Hallowe'en. She
had bought Gavin a fancy clown suit trimmed with
yards of orange and green ruffles. A bright orange wig
went with it. After dinner on Hallowe'en night, she
painted Gavin's face with rouge and white make-up.

"Doesn't he look precious, Mary?" Aunt Florence
held Gavin out at arm's length, then kissed him. "Now
I'll take your picture and send it to your parents. Come
along, Norah, you get in it too."

Aunt Mary had helped Norah find some old
clothes. She wore a pair of Hugh's tattered fishing
pants, a shapeless shirt and Mr Ogilvie's felt hat. With
glee at being allowed to be so messy, she'd daubed her
face and hands with a burnt cork.

"Don't stand too close to Gavin," warned Aunt
Florence. "You might get him dirty." She focused the
camera on them. "There!"

Norah blinked from the flash as the front door
knocker sounded. Into the hall walked another tramp,

a witch and a black cat with a bedraggled tail: Paige, Barbara and Daphne.

"I want you back by nine o'clock, Norah," said Aunt Florence. "I'll lend you my watch. Do you have rules about where you're allowed to go, Paige?"

"Yes, Mrs Ogilvie," said Paige politely. "We aren't allowed to cross Yonge Street." She winked at Norah when Aunt Florence's back was turned.

"Let's go, then, Gavin." Aunt Florence was planning to drive him around to all her friends' houses. His cheerful wig and make-up were a sharp contrast to his doleful expression. He turned to Norah and said plaintively, "Can't I come with you, instead?"

"You're too young," muttered Norah.

"Of course not, sweetness," agreed Aunt Florence. "You'd have trouble trying to keep up."

"Why can't he?" asked Paige. "We'll take care of him."

"Thank you, Paige, but I don't think he'd enjoy it." Gavin looked back longingly as Aunt Florence led him away.

Norah was surprised he wanted to come; she thought he was afraid of the Worsleys. But she forgot his hurt face when they went out into the street. Shadowy figures hurried past them in the darkness: ghosts, cowboys, pilots, soldiers and pirates. A spooky breeze swirled dead leaves around their feet. They met Bernard, as planned, at the corner. He made an odd-looking tramp in his glasses.

"*Shell out! Shell out! The witches are out!*" The thin cry echoed around them as gangs of purposeful

children tramped up the steps of houses lit with leering pumpkin faces.

In school they had been asked to collect pennies
instead of candy for the war effort, but they carried pil-
lowcases along with their milk bottles. At almost every
door they received a treat as well as a donation.

Paige refused to ask for money. "It's not fair. I've already collected the most bottle caps in my class for the
Red Cross. Tonight's supposed to be *our* night! If they
don't give us any candy, we'll play tricks on them."

"Like what?" asked Norah.

"Like soaping their windows or taking off their
gates or filling their mailboxes with horse buns," said
Paige. "At least, that's what the older kids do. I've never
actually done a trick — but that doesn't mean I
wouldn't."

They crossed Yonge Street to cover Bernard's
neighbourhood as well. On one corner Charlie and his
friends were noisily overturning garbage cans. They
watched from a distance, careful to stay far enough
away to run. Then they dared one another to ring the
bell of an unlit old house. Daphne was the only one
brave enough, but no one answered.

"Hello, Norah!" Norah jumped as a white gloved
hand tapped her shoulder. It was Dulcie, in a lacy dress
and jewels. Her face was thick with make-up.

"Isn't Hallowe'en super? We're all film stars — I'm
Betty Grable." Behind her lurked Babs and Ernestine,
their galoshes peeking out from under their long
gowns.

Babs frowned at Norah and Bernard. "Come *on*

Dulcie, we have to go home now."

"*We* refused to accept candy," said Ernestine righteously, at the sight of Norah's bulging pillowcase. "You're supposed to be collecting money."

"I did!" Norah shook her bottle of coins angrily.

"*Dulcie . . .* " Babs was moving away. "Don't you remember the party at my house? Mum's made scads of fudge, and we're going to bob for apples — you'll like that."

Dulcie hesitated. "I don't feel like going in yet. You go ahead. I'll see you there."

Her friends looked surprised but left quickly. Dulcie seemed surprised herself at her daring. "Can I come with you for a while?" she asked timidly.

Norah grinned. "Sure!" She introduced Dulcie to the Worsleys. Paige inspected her warily, but soon forgot Dulcie as they collected more candy.

When their bags were almost too heavy to carry, they rested under a streetlight and compared their booty. Best were homemade popcorn balls; worst were ordinary apples you could get anytime.

"We still have an hour before we have to go home," said Paige, pulling out a long string of toffee from her teeth. "I know something you'd like, Norah. Why don't we have a bonfire? Then we could celebrate Guy Fawkes too."

"But we don't have a Guy!" said Norah.

"And we don't have matches," said Bernard, looking worried. "Anyway there's nowhere safe to make a fire."

But Paige, as usual, was unstoppable when she

had an idea. "I took some matches from the living room before we left. And I have a Guy." Out of her pocket she pulled a small, wilted rag doll. "It isn't very big, but it'll do."

"That's mine!" protested Daphne.

"You haven't played with it for years — you never did. It doesn't even have a name. Wouldn't you like to see it burn up?"

Daphne thought for a second and then nodded, a wicked gleam in her eye.

Up to now, Dulcie had seemed to be enjoying herself. Now she looked scared. "I think I'll go to the party, now — Babs's house is just around the corner." She hurried away.

"She's a chicken," remarked Paige, digging in her pockets again.

Norah thought of how Dulcie had done what she wanted in spite of her friends' disapproval. "No, she's not. She likes doing different things than us, but she's all right really."

"If you say so. Now watch." She had found a pencil and marked a moustache under the doll's nose. "There, we'll turn him into Hitler — then it will be even more fun to burn him. We'll make the fire by the fort. If we pile dirt around it, it'll be safe. Come on, while we still have time!"

Bernard still looked reluctant and Norah felt a twinge of fear. But the Worsley girls were at their wildest. They whooped and pranced as they ran along the streets and into the ravine. It was difficult to find their way to the fort in the darkness and they held onto one another as they slithered down the bank. Gradually their eyes adjusted and they could see by the dim glow of the streetlights on the bridge above them.

"I'm freezing!" complained Barbara. "Hurry and make the fire, Paige."

First Paige ordered them to gather up twigs and branches while she and Bernard dug a circular trench with a board from the fort. When they had a large pile of fuel she struck a match on a rock and held it to the smallest twigs.

The flame flickered and went out. Norah breathed easily again, but Paige looked around impatiently. "Paper . . . that's what we need. Can we use some old comics? We've read them all."

Before they could answer she had grabbed an armful of comics from the fort. She tore out the pages, wadded them up, fit them under the kindling and tried again.

The wind rose and the paper caught at once and whooshed into a blaze. Soon the twigs ignited, then the larger branches. The sparks flew up into the darkness and the dancing yellow flames illuminated their grimy faces.

"Yaaay!" Paige threw the doll into the fire and seized Norah's hand. Hollering like banshees, they all circled the flames as they grew stronger.

The crackling fire made Norah feel reckless and powerful. She stopped being afraid. She almost forgot she was in Canada and for a few seconds was at home in Ringden before the war, dancing around the Guy.

Guy, Guy, Guy
Poke him in the eye.
Put him in the fire
And there let him die.
Burn his body from his head,
Then you'll say Guy Fawkes is dead.
Hip, Hip, Hooray!

The others joined in with her chant. "Then you'll say that *Hitler's* dead!" added Paige. The flames leapt defiantly and they hurled wood on the fire to feed its mounting rage. Even Bernard had lost his usual calm. "This is Charlie!" he shouted, throwing on a large branch.

Norah added more comics. "And this is Aunt Florence!" she screamed. Even Paige looked a little shocked at that. Then she grinned and shouted, "School! Dresses! GROWN-UPS!" They circled and jumped and shrieked, the fire roaring with them.

Suddenly Bernard gave a different kind of scream. "LOOK!" He pointed and they froze. Part of the fire had leapt across the trench and caught on one of the cardboard boxes they used as a table. The dry box flared instantly and then the flames travelled to the fort itself.

"Stop it!" cried Paige. "Put dirt on it!"

They threw on handfuls of dirt and tried to beat down the flames with branches. But the fire continued to snarl like an angry beast at the wood of the fort.

Daphne sobbed hysterically and Barbara clung to her, her face white with terror. "*Do* something!" she entreated the older children.

Bernard turned to Norah. "Run up to the Ogilvies' and call the fire department. Hurry! Paige and I will keep throwing dirt on it."

Norah didn't know how she made her legs work. She tripped and stumbled up the steep bank. When she reached the front door, she felt as if she were suffocating and struggled for air.

"Norah! What's wrong?" Aunt Mary sprang up as Norah appeared in the den.

"Fire. In the ravine," Norah gasped. "The others — are — down there." Then her arms and legs turned boneless and she collapsed in a chair.

The rest of the evening had the foggy, unreal quality of a dream. The fire engines came quickly, their whining wail as insistent as an air-raid siren. In a daze, Norah stood in the backyard and watched as long hoses sprayed onto the flames from the bridge. The firemen led or carried Paige, Bernard, Barbara and Daphne up the hill as the fire was extinguished.

None of them could speak. When Aunt Florence and Gavin got home, all five children were sitting in the kitchen, with Aunt Mary and Hanny trying to get them to have some cocoa. The firemen were standing in a corner drinking theirs, looking sternly at the children.

"*What* is going on?" the majestic voice asked. Aunt Florence directed her question to Norah, after glaring first at Bernard.

Fortunately Mr Worsley arrived before Norah had to answer. "Are you all right?" he cried, inspecting each daughter as if she might be broken. Then he looked grave. He said he would drive Bernard home and hustled him and his daughters out the door.

"Obviously there's a lot of explaining to do," he said to Aunt Florence, "but I think it can wait until tomorrow. They'd all better stay home from school. I'll ring you in the morning and we'll try to sort out what happened."

Norah was sent to bed. She didn't even wash her filthy face and hands but curled up into a tight ball and tried to quiet her breathing. The dangerous, leaping flames and Aunt Florence's outraged expression filled her dreams.

The next morning, it all came out. The Worsleys arrived after breakfast and the girls had to stumble through the story together in front of the four adults.

Aunt Florence blamed a lot of it on Bernard. "I told you he was unsuitable! And why were you with him at all, Norah, after I forbade you to see him?"

Then she discovered that Norah had been seeing Bernard all along. "We didn't know she wasn't allowed to play with him," said Mrs Worsley timidly. "We thought his name was Albert. He seems so sensible for his age, it couldn't have been his idea."

"It was *my* idea," said Paige. "Not Bernard's."

"I'm sure it was," said her father grimly.

But Aunt Florence didn't seem to believe her. "Now, Paige, you couldn't have thought of such a dreadful thing by yourself. And it was extremely deceptive of you, Norah, to pretend Bernard was someone else."

Mr Worsley gave them a long, serious lecture on

how foolish they had been. He told them exactly the same sorts of things Norah's father would have. It was painful to listen to — Barbara cried and Paige pressed her lips together and pretended not to — but everything he said was so true that Norah felt cleansed at the end.

Then Mrs Worsley and Aunt Mary had their turn. They wrung their hands and carried on about how they might have been burnt to death. Then Norah and Paige were told they weren't allowed to see each other all weekend.

Throughout all this, Aunt Florence was suspiciously silent. Norah guessed she was saving the rest of her comments for her alone.

Sure enough, after Paige, Barbara and Daphne had been marched home again, Aunt Florence had her say. She kept Norah in the living room for half an hour and told her over and over how ungrateful and disobedient she was.

She even brought up Norah's bed-wetting. Before breakfast, as if she had decided to pick a time when Norah was already in everyone's bad books, Edith had come to Aunt Florence to tell her she refused to wash Norah's sheets any longer.

"What kind of a girl wets her bed at age ten?" said Aunt Florence, looking disgusted. "I think you must be doing it on purpose."

The more her icy voice droned on, the less Norah listened. Something inside her had turned to stone.

"Norah! I said, would you like me to have you transferred to another family? I'm not at all sure I want to continue to try to get along, when you make absolutely no effort yourself. I'm not even sure that Gavin should be around you. Perhaps you would be better apart."

Norah fastened her own grey eyes upon Aunt Florence's granite ones. "I don't care. Do whatever you like. May I go to my room now?"

Aunt Florence seemed about to say more. Then she took a deep breath and nodded. "Very well. We'll discuss this again later, when we've both cooled down. You'd better go to school this afternoon. Wash your hands for lunch and I'll write you a note."

Norah sat on the window seat of the tower. She struggled through five short minutes of indecision, then she dumped her books out of her schoolbag and began to pack.

XIX

Gavin

"Are you sure you feel up to going back to school this afternoon, Norah?" Aunt Mary asked anxiously. She adjusted her hat at the hall mirror. "You must still feel shocked from last night — I know I do."

Her mother bristled. "Of course she can go back. There's no point in missing a whole day of schoolwork. Why are you wearing that dreadful hat, Mary? Go and put on your new one." She and her daughter were going to a lunch party.

Before Aunt Mary scuttled upstairs, Norah tried to smile at her. Then she met Aunt Florence's haughty gaze with one just as cold. There! That was the last time she would ever see either of them.

"I'm glad you didn't get burned up, Norah," said Gavin, as they ate alone at one end of the dining room table.

Norah was too distracted to listen. "Aren't you

going to finish your sandwich?" When Gavin shook his head, she stuffed the remains of his lunch and three of the apples from the sideboard into her schoolbag.

"What's that for?" asked Gavin.

"Just a . . . picnic. We're having one after school. But don't tell, or I'll get into trouble."

"I won't. Can I come? Will you have it in your fort? When did you build the fort? Can I help you fix it?"

"No you *can't*! Leave me alone, Gavin! Why do you always have to bother me? Can't you see I'm trying to think? Go and find Hanny — I'm going to school now."

Gavin's big eyes filled with tears. Slowly he got down from his chair and trudged into the kitchen.

Norah almost cried herself, with frustration. Why did Gavin always have to make her feel so mean? And shouldn't she say goodbye to him? She wouldn't see him again until the war was over and he was sent back to England. It would just upset him, though, if she told him she was running away. He might even tell the Ogilvies.

The front hall was as soundless as an empty church. Norah pulled down her new snowsuit from the closet and struggled into the leggings and jacket. The weather wasn't cold today, but she didn't know where she would be spending the night. She checked her schoolbag one more time: toothbrush, pyjamas, an extra sweater and her shrapnel; the five pounds she'd held onto all this time and, for some reason, the old doll Aunt Mary had given her. She'd also squeezed in her latest library book. That felt like stealing, but she could mail it back from England.

She breathed in one last whiff of furniture polish and roses and said a silent goodbye to the sombre house that always felt too hot. Then she shut the door softly behind her.

It was difficult to walk fast in the bulky snowsuit. Norah decided to inspect the fort and rest there until she calmed down. This was much scarier than skipping school; scarier, in fact, than anything she'd ever done before.

In the sunlight the charred wood of the fort looked sinister. But the damage wasn't as bad as it had appeared to be last night. Norah sat down beside the damp, sooty circle where they'd made the fire. It seemed years ago that they had all danced around the flames.

She tried to think clearly. Where was she going to go? All she knew was that she wanted to go home, to find her way back to England and her parents. The only way she could do that was to return the way she had come: by train to Montreal and from there by ship. First she had to find the train station; that shouldn't be too difficult. She remembered it was a short distance from the university. She could go downtown and ask someone.

But adults might question her and wonder why she wasn't in school. Could she get away with travelling alone on a train? And how was she going to find out what ship to go on? Would she have to stow away on it, like someone in a story?

The load of all the problems that lay ahead overwhelmed her. She had not slept well the night before and the horror of the fire had left her drained. It was unusually warm for November; her snowsuit was a cosy cocoon. Curling up on a heap of dry leaves, Norah slept.

She dreamed about journeys, about walking and walking and walking with no place to reach. As she walked she held a small warm hand that gave her strength. She was in England; she was walking with Gavin. The sense of endless journeying left when they approached their own village. As they hurried up the main street to their house, a huge relief flowed through Norah. She began to run, pulling Gavin along and laughing in anticipation of feeling her parents' arms around her.

But Little Whitebull was demolished. In its place was a pile of burnt and flattened rubble — like the fort, like Grandad's house in Camber.

"Where are you?" Norah cried desperately. "Mum! Dad! Grandad! Where are you?"

"They're gone..." cackled an ugly voice. It was a goblin voice, a bogeyman, a Guy . . . coming from a leering face with a brush of a moustache and a swastika on its hat. It leaned over her and laughed raucously. "They're *gone*, they're *dead* . . . I killed them!"

"*No!*" screamed Norah and woke herself up. She sat up with a jolt and sobbed. It was only a dream, but she couldn't stop crying for a long time.

Now she wanted to reach England all the more, to make sure her family was safe. Why was she wasting time down here? She stood up, brushed off the leaves, picked up her schoolbag and reached out for Gavin's hand.

Her hand closed on air. She thrust it into her pocket angrily. Gavin was still at the Ogilvies', being cosseted and spoilt. She didn't want or need him.

Then her legs trembled so much she had to sit down again, as everyone's words came to her; "Take care of Gavin, take care of Gavin . . . "

She had *never* taken care of him. From the very beginning of their journey to Canada, she had only wanted to be rid of him. She remembered all the times when he'd given her that hurt, perplexed look; all the times she could have comforted him, but didn't. And the last time, a few hours ago, when she'd made him cry by pushing him away. He was only five, a small, lost boy with no family but her. He was her brother; Aunt Mary and Bernard and Paige didn't have brothers. She thought of Aunt Mary's anguished voice when she had talked about Hugh. She had lost her brother; Norah still had hers.

She remembered the day, years ago, when they'd set Gavin on one side of the kitchen at Little Whitebull and, chortling with proud glee, he'd taken his first wobbly steps straight to Norah. How he used to call "Ora, Ora," when Mum scolded him. But she had only thought of him as a nuisance; someone who claimed her mother's and sisters' attention so completely that she had turned to her father instead.

But he was her brother. He needed Norah and Norah needed him. And she was planning to leave him behind in a strange country with a foolish woman to ruin him.

Norah ran up the hill almost as fast as she had the night before. She tried to catch her breath as she pushed open the front door a crack and peeked in.

Good: the hall clock said just past two. She hadn't slept as long as she thought. And Gavin, as usual, was playing in the hall with the canes and umbrellas that had once belonged to Mr Ogilvie — patting and grooming and talking to them quietly, pretending they were horses.

Norah watched him for a moment. She saw his dreamy, withdrawn expression, his aloneness. What had it been like for him these past two months, shut up in this dull house by himself when Aunt Florence was busy? She wanted to rush up and greet him noisily; she felt as if she hadn't seen him for years.

But she had to be cautious. "Gavin," she whispered.

Gavin dropped a cane, startled.

"Shhh! It's only me. Come on, we're going out." Norah crept into the hall and got his snowsuit.

"Going out? With *you*?" His face was so eager that Norah hugged him.

"Yes. We're running away. But they might try to stop us, so we have to be quiet. What's Hanny doing?"

"Making a pie. She's going to call when it's done so I can have a piece."

Norah could smell it cooking. "Then hurry!" She helped him into his leggings. "I wish we could get more food and your toothbrush, but there isn't time. Do you have Creature?"

Gavin held up his elephant, his eyes shining. "We're having an adventure, aren't we?"

"Right. Come on, now." With her brother's warm hand firmly in hers, Norah led him out the door.

Five hours later, they sat huddled on a hard bench hidden behind a bush in a park close to the train station. A nearby streetlight radiated a faint circle of light.

Norah sat in the light, reading aloud from *Five Children and It*: " 'I daresay you have often thought about what you would do if you had three wishes given you.' " When she reached the part where the children couldn't decide what to wish for, she turned the book over impatiently. *Her* wish was so simple, but bringing it about seemed increasingly complicated.

The temperature had dropped and now she was glad of their snowsuits. Gavin's cheeks and nose were cherry-red with cold. "Keep reading, Norah," he begged. "I like that funny Psammead."

"In a minute — I have to think. You go and swing for a while, it will warm you up."

Gavin obeyed easily. He was so contented to be doing something with Norah that he didn't seem to mind the hours they had already spent walking and waiting.

First they'd gone downtown and ventured into the bank to change the five pounds.

"Where did you get this?" the teller asked suspiciously. "It's a large amount for a little girl."

"Our m-mum sent us with it — she's ill," stuttered Norah, feeling a bit ill herself with the huge lie.

The teller still looked suspicious but she finally handed Norah a wad of Canadian dollars.

After that they had asked a boy the way to Union Station and gone there on a streetcar. Norah was afraid to call more attention to themselves by asking about the train to Montreal. She finally found a schedule on a notice-board; to her dismay, the next train didn't leave until eight-thirty that evening.

They passed the time by buying tea and cheese sandwiches in the station restaurant. The cashier looked at them curiously but she didn't say anything. Then they settled themselves on a long, slippery bench in the echoing station hall. They took off their snowsuits and leaned comfortably against them. The station milled with weekend travellers, but they were all preoccupied with where they were going or whom they were meeting. No one paid any attention to Norah and Gavin until a policeman approached them.

"Are you kids alone?" he asked kindly, with an English accent.

Norah thought fast. "No, our mum's gone to get us some sandwiches. We have to wait a long time for the train."

"Where are you off to, then?"

"Montreal. We're going to visit some friends of Mum's for the weekend."

"War guests, are you?"

Norah nodded.

"You're lucky your mother could come over with

you. I have a sister and three nephews back home I wanted to bring to Canada, but it's too late now. Since that ship was torpedoed, they've suspended all evacuation indefinitely. Where are you from? I grew up in Newcastle."

Norah told him. He was so friendly she wanted to pour out everything, but that was impossible. And the longer he chatted, the sooner he would wonder where their mother was. At least Gavin knew enough not to contradict her story.

She became more and more agitated. Then, to her relief, a drunken man shouting on the other side of the station caught the policeman's attention.

"I'll have to check this out. Now don't move from that bench. I'm sure your mother will be back soon."

As soon as he'd left Norah grabbed their things and pulled Gavin outside. "Where are we going?" he asked, as they hid behind a pillar and struggled into their snowsuits.

"I don't know. We'll just have to keep walking until it's time to buy our tickets. If we sit down we look too conspicuous."

So they walked and walked again until their legs ached, peering into store windows and warming up in the lobby of an enormous hotel. When it got dark they were less visible, but the lights of the passing cars glared in their faces and made them jumpy. Finally they found the park and settled on the half-hidden bench.

Now Norah watched Gavin pumping hard, his body a darting shadow in the darkness. It was too cold to stay here much longer; they should probably start back to the station.

She dreaded trying to buy a ticket. What would she say? She was certain they wouldn't sell her one, and perhaps the policeman would be waiting for them.

Something firm and resolute collapsed inside Norah. She had rescued Gavin from the Ogilvies; to carry on from there seemed impossible. She was only ten years old — the grown-ups would thwart her all the way. However much she wanted to, she had known all along they couldn't really go back to England.

They were stuck here; stuck in Canada with no place to go. Just as at the beginning of her dream, they were on a journey with no end in sight.

Gavin jumped off the swing and ran back to Norah. "I'm much warmer now, but I'm hungry again. Can I have my sandwich from lunch? Norah? Why are you crying?"

Norah's body heaved with sobs and hot tears stung her cold cheeks. "I'm so tired," she wailed. "I'm tired of — of fighting. Why does there have to be a war? I *hate* the war! I just want to go *home*."

Gavin thumped her back. "Let's go then," he said calmly. "Aunt Florence will wonder where we are. I don't think she'd like it if we ran away without telling her. And there's apple pie for dessert."

Norah was so surprised she stopped crying. "I don't mean the *Ogilvies*. I mean home! In Ringden, with Mum and Dad and Grandad. In *England*. Don't you remember?"

" 'Course I remember. But I thought Canada was our home now."

Norah stared at him. "Gavin, do you like living at the Ogilvies'?"

"I like Aunt Florence and Aunt Mary and Hanny and all my new toys. But I don't like shopping and going out for tea all the time. I wish I could go to school like you."

"But you came with me when I said we were running away!"

"You said we were going to have an adventure. But we didn't even go on a train and I thought we'd be finished the adventure by dinnertime. I'm tired of it now. Can't we go home? Please?"

Norah gave up. There was nowhere else to go but the Ogilvies'. "All right," she said wearily, drying her wet cheeks with her mitt. "We'll get into a lot of trouble, though. I will, anyway. Probably they'll send me to a different family." She stood up. "But I won't go without you! Would you mind that, if we had to live with someone else?"

"I wouldn't like it," said Gavin gravely, "but I'd go with you. Dad said we had to stick to each other like glue!"

Norah had to smile at his serious expression. "He was right — from now on, we will."

"Come on." Gavin took her hand and pulled her out of the park. "Maybe there'll be some pie left."

People stared at them on the streetcar, but no one asked questions. When they finally reached the Ogilvies' house they found it blazing with lights. A police car was parked outside.

"Uh-oh." Norah paused a minute and gathered up the last shreds of her courage. This was going to be much more difficult than watching the sky for paratroopers. She was so worn out, she wondered if she could make it up the steps. "All right . . . let's get it over with."

They pushed open the front door and stood in the entrance of the living room, hand in hand. A noisy rush of bodies descended on them. Hanny squealed and Aunt Mary kissed them again and again. Mrs Worsley wept. Mr Worsley kept ruffling Norah's hair repeating, "Well! You're safe! Well, well!" Even Paige and Dulcie were there, jumping up and down and pulling on Norah's arms.

They were glad to see her! thought Norah with tired surprise. Everyone was hugging and kissing her. No one was angry. She felt as slack as a rag doll, as she was passed from arm to arm.

Then she stiffened. Aunt Florence had Gavin enveloped in her embrace. "Oh, my sweetness, are you all right? Are you sure?" She released him gently and turned to face Norah. For a few seconds the two of them stared awkwardly at each other.

"Are you going to send me away?" whispered Norah.

"Send you away?" To Norah's astonishment, Aunt Florence's eyes were swimming in tears. But they were probably only left over from greeting Gavin.

Her strong voice faltered, though, as she continued. "I will *never* send you away, Norah. You're one of the family. I want to apologize for what I said this morning. Will you forgive me? Will you let me have another chance?"

Everyone, including Norah, was silenced by this humility. Aunt Florence put out her hand. Norah hesitated for only an instant, then she took it in her own. She kept hold of the firm grasp as her eyes closed; Aunt Florence caught her before she reached the floor.

Part Three

XX

Beginning Again

Norah turned over and stretched. Her arm was in a warm puddle of sunshine. She sat up and peeked through the half-open curtains. The sun was high; she must have slept most of the morning. But it was Saturday, she remembered, and delicious to lie here doing nothing.

Then she grinned; her bed was dry. A strange tranquillity filled her from head to toe. She didn't understand it; shouldn't she be in trouble, after all that had happened yesterday?

She got up to go to the bathroom, then luxuriated in bed again. A tantalizing smell of bacon drifted up the stairs. Norah tensed again, as uncertain about what to do next as on her first day in the house. Perhaps she was going to be punished, in spite of her reception last night.

There was a knock on her door and Aunt Florence

strode in, carrying a tray. "Are you awake now? You've had a good long sleep. You're to eat up all of this and spend the next two days in bed. Did you know that you fainted last night?"

Norah couldn't remember. She dug into the scrambled eggs, bacon and toast, while Aunt Florence told her how Dr Morris had come and said she was over-tired and strained. With awe, Norah watched Aunt Florence swish open the curtains and hang up Norah's clothes. She had never come up here before.

"All finished? Good girl. Now, Norah, there are a few things I want to say about last night — then we'll consider the matter closed. I think you must know what a foolish thing it was to wander around the city on your own, especially with your little brother in your charge. Do you promise never to do such a thing again?"

Norah nodded.

"Very well. Do you recall what I said last night?" Another nod. They both looked embarrassed.

"I meant it. After we discovered you were gone Mary told me, in no uncertain terms" — Aunt Florence grimaced, as if she were still in shock — "that it was my fault you ran away. She was right, Norah. I've been so wrapped up with Gavin, I've paid no attention to *you*. Perhaps we are too much alike, you and I. That doesn't mean we can't try to get along." She paused awkwardly and took the tray over to the table. Then she stood and stared out the window.

Norah looked at her strong back, knowing she should speak but tongue-tied with mixed feelings.

Imagine Aunt Mary saying that to her mother!

Was it Aunt Florence's fault? Not entirely, she thought uncomfortably. She had set herself against Aunt Florence from the start. Aunt Florence had been just as pigheaded. Now, though, she was giving in first.

"Norah?" The majestic figure turned around and faced the bed. "What do you think? I'm willing to begin again if you are."

Norah knew how hard it was for her to say that. She smiled apprehensively. "So am I," she whispered.

"Good! You know, my dear . . . until you left . . . I didn't realize how . . . how fond of you I am." She walked over and gave Norah a firm kiss on her forehead. Then she sat down on the bed and said, as if nothing had happened, "Now then, would you like me to read to you?"

With relief they both escaped into the safe world of *Five Children and It*. Norah only half-listened. Aunt Florence had kissed her! She felt as if she hadn't woken up yet.

Gavin wandered in and curled up on the end of the bed; then Aunt Mary came up to collect the tray. It was strange, but pleasant, to have so many people in the room that had been her solitary retreat for so long.

Norah was left alone to rest. She snuggled under the eiderdown and thought hard all afternoon. Last night Aunt Florence had asked for "another chance". It looked as if Norah were being given another chance as well. She could begin all over again, as though she had just come to Canada.

The rest of the weekend was punctuated by trays of food, visitors, books and naps. Norah lazed in bed and made plans. By Sunday evening she was refreshed and strong, with her new resolutions all ready.

She began at breakfast on Monday morning, after Aunt Florence had appeared at the table unexpectedly. "I decided to let Mary sleep in for a change," she explained.

"Gavin is going to school with me today," Norah announced.

"*Am* I?" cried Gavin eagerly.

"But . . . " Aunt Florence started to frown, then she seemed to remember *her* new self and continued in a more controlled tone. "Now, Norah, I agree that, since he's almost six, he's ready for school. But I planned to enroll him at St Martin's. It's a small private school that will suit him much better than Prince Edward. And I was thinking that after Christmas you could go to Brackley Hall with Paige. Wouldn't you like that? I would pay for both, of course."

Norah tried to speak as politely as possible. "Thank you, Aunt Florence, but I think we should both go to the same school so I can keep an eye on him." She looked Aunt Florence in the eye. "I'm sure that's what my parents would want."

This was a conflict conducted on different terms than before — being civilized instead of out of control. Norah sat up straighter, enjoying herself. She knew she was going to win.

Aunt Florence hesitated, then smiled slightly. "Very

well, if you think that's best, Norah. But he doesn't
need to start now. He can wait till after Christmas."

"Oh, Aunt Florence, don't you think he might start
now?" said Norah patiently. "He's missed so much
already. I would hate to have to tell Mum and Dad how
much he's missed." She put down her orange juice
glass and waited.

Aunt Florence gave one last try. "Maybe we should
ask Gavin. Would you like to go to school, sweetness?
To Norah's school, or to a nice private school?"

"To Norah's!" said Gavin loudly.

"All right," sighed Aunt Florence, "but wouldn't
you rather wait until January? Don't forget, we were
going to visit Mrs Teagle today. You know how much
you like her cat."

"I want to go now!" Gavin was so excited he tipped
his chair backwards and almost fell off it.

With an odd, surprised look at Norah, Aunt
Florence sighed again. "If that's what you want, then
you can. I'll phone Mr Evans and tell him you're
coming this morning with Norah."

Norah hadn't told Aunt Florence how worried she was
that Gavin would be as estranged as she was at school.
There were several other war guests in grade one,
however; he wouldn't stand out like her. When she
checked on him at recess, Gavin was holding out his
cupped palms while another small boy poured
something into them. "Hello, Norah," he called. "Dick's
trading these wizard marbles for one of my soldiers."
He pocketed the marbles and ran off with Dick after a

football.

Norah went to find Bernard by the flagpole. They had a lot to talk about; she hadn't seen him since the night of the fire.

"Where did you go on Friday?" he asked immediately. "Mrs Ogilvie rang our house to see if you were there."

"I'd rather not talk about it," mumbled Norah. Bernard seemed to understand; they discussed Hallowe'en night instead, reviewing all the horrifying details. "Mum was so upset she cried," said Bernard quietly.

"Would you like to come over after school?" Norah asked, when the bell rang. "Paige is going to meet us there after her piano lesson."

"I thought I wasn't allowed to!"

"Don't worry — things have changed."

As the three of them — Norah, Bernard and Gavin — walked home that afternoon, Norah wondered if she were pushing her luck. But she felt strong enough for another battle and took Bernard directly into the den.

"I've brought Bernard home," she said. "Can we ask Hanny for a snack?"

Aunt Florence looked up from her needlepoint; her arm jerked with surprise. "Bernard? Now, Norah . . . " She stopped and took a breath. "Uhhh . . . does your mother know you're here, Bernard?"

"Yes, Mrs Ogilvie," said Bernard, trying to hide behind Norah.

Aunt Florence continued to stare at him and Norah felt sorry for her. "Can we have a snack?" she asked again gently.

"I suppose so . . . go into the kitchen and get something." She still looked bewildered as they left the room.

Aunt Florence never said anything to Norah about inviting Bernard over; but after that, whenever he came, she treated him with stiff politeness. Norah was grateful; she knew that was the best she could do.

Instead of being marooned up in her tower, Norah began to wander almost as freely over the Ogilvies' house as in her own. She even went into Aunt Mary's bedroom sometimes, talking to her as she got dressed to go out. Aunt Mary let her try on her jewellery and her many hats. The only room Norah didn't venture into was Aunt Florence's; that would be going too far.

Norah also began to spend time in the kitchen again and no one objected. "Mary and Hugh used to visit me like this," said Hanny. "I wondered why you stayed away."

"But Aunt Florence said I was bothering you!"

"Oh, *her*. You'll soon learn she doesn't mean half the things she says. If I believed her, I would have been let go a hundred times over. The trouble with that one is she speaks before she thinks. I always just listen politely and do what I want. She knows I will, or I wouldn't stay."

Hanny was right. To win with Aunt Florence, you had to be just as forthright as she was. Her and Norah's personalities still clashed, but their relationship had changed, as if each had a secret respect for the other.

Now Bernard and Paige sometimes played at Norah's house. Gavin often tagged along and got used to being an extra in their games. School made him braver; sometimes when they went to the Worsleys' he would fight back when Daphne and Barbara teased him.

Norah began to feel as proud of Gavin as Aunt Florence was. "He's a very clever little boy," Mrs Ogilvie boasted. "His teacher tells me he's way ahead of the rest of the class."

Norah took him to the library and introduced him to Miss Gleeson. "I didn't know you had a little brother!" the librarian beamed. "Why haven't you brought him before?"

"He was . . . um . . . busy," mumbled Norah, her cheeks red. "He can read very well for his age. Have you any easy books?"

Norah still didn't know what to do about school — how to tackle the problem of her classmates' indifference or Miss Liers's hostility. She wondered if it would be any better if she *did* go to Paige's school; but she knew she couldn't desert Gavin or Bernard. By now she was quite used to being isolated, but she still watched the playground games longingly and wished for more friends. Everyone seemed to have forgotten about her, even Charlie's gang.

Each Tuesday morning Miss Liers took a few minutes to write the war news on the board and ask for contributions. Before, Norah had never offered any. Instead she would stare haughtily into space and think about how much more she knew about the war than the others did.

A few days after Coventry was bombed, she sat in silence while Miss Liers described the damage in sober tones.

"I saw bombs like that on a news-reel — they can flatten a whole town!" said Charlie. He gave a wailing screech and crashed his hand on his desk.

If the Nazis could do so much to large places like Coventry and London, what would they do to Ringden? Norah's chest felt heavy. She looked across at Dulcie and saw that she was pale and silent.

Charlie kept on describing the bombs with gusto, getting more and more lurid. Suddenly Norah couldn't stand it any more.

"Stop!" she cried, turning around to face him. "You don't even know what it's like! What about the *people*? My grandfather's house was smashed by a bomb. He was just lucky he wasn't in it." She shuddered, remembering her dream.

"Norah is right, Charlie," said Miss Liers. "You are so far away from the war, you find it exciting. But war isn't a game — it's a grim, terrible thing." For once, her voice wasn't sarcastic. She looked at Norah with respect for the first time since she'd read aloud the poem that first week of school. "Would you like to tell us more about what it was like? Come and stand at the front and see how much you can remember."

Norah didn't want to be on display in front of the whole class, but she had to do as she was told. She drew courage from glancing at Princess Margaret Rose in the picture at the front of the room, then began slowly with last May and Dunkirk. She told them how thousands of British troops had been rescued from France by small civilian boats, and how she and Molly had stood by the railway tracks for days, waving to the trains of exhausted soldiers coming from the coast.

Her voice grew more confident as she described how the village had prepared for an invasion; she began to enjoy herself and chose her words with relish. As her story became more exciting she spoke louder and faster. The class was as transfixed as when the librarian had told "Alenoushka". Norah related all the details about the dogfights, the parachutes, the Boot and all the other things that had dropped out of the sky. When she reached the part about the crashed plane her words rushed out with a power that seemed to belong to someone else.

Then Charlie thrust up his hand, startling Norah from the spell she was casting. The others scowled at him for interrupting. "Miss Liers, that couldn't be true, could it?"

Miss Liers frowned at him. "Of course it's true, Charlie. Do you think Norah would lie to us? I thought you knew all about the war. Maybe you should start reading the papers, as well as going to the movies. Let Norah finish, please."

Abashed, Charlie kept quiet. Norah talked all the way through the first period, when they were supposed to be having arithmetic. Even Dulcie looked awed, as if the things Norah was describing hadn't happened to her as well. After Norah reached the part about arriving in Toronto she stopped, as drained as if she had experienced the whole journey again.

Miss Liers actually smiled. "Thank you, Norah, that was *very* interesting. We're glad that you and Dulcie are safe in Canada." For once, she didn't remind the class of all the children who weren't.

At recess Norah was surrounded by questioners, just as Dulcie had been on their first day. Charlie even asked her if he could see her shrapnel. When Norah brought it back after lunch, the grade sixes came over to admire it as well.

Norah thought that after that she would be popular again. But although people were friendly to her now, she was still barred from the activities she liked. In this school, the unspoken rule about boys never associating with girls was never broken. When she asked the boys if she could be in their football game, they just muttered, "Girls don't *play* football," and looked embarrassed.

Instead, she sometimes joined the girls' skipping. She learnt a lot of new rhymes: "I love coffee/I love tea", "Dancing Dolly" and "Yoki and the Kaiser". But when she played with the girls she felt guilty for abandoning Bernard. He was still bullied, especially if Norah wasn't with him.

"Can't you leave him alone?" Norah yelled at Charlie, when they had painted a swastika on his bike.

"You don't understand," said Charlie, running away before Norah could argue.

"We should tell Mr Evans!" said Norah, but

Bernard wouldn't let her.

"He knows. He's even spoken to Charlie, but that doesn't do any good." Bernard tried to scrape off the black cross on his fender. "Do you think Paige has any paint I can cover this with?"

Norah kicked the frozen ground angrily. There were some things she could not change.

The weather became so cold that part of the school playground was sprayed with hoses and turned into a skating rink. Aunt Mary took Norah and Gavin down to the basement, where she opened a cupboard crammed with skates, skis and hockey sticks. "I'm sure we can find some to fit you," she said. "Look, these must be your size, Norah."

The black, lace-up boots had shiny blades attached. For Gavin there were double-edged skates that fastened to his galoshes. Aunt Mary dusted off her own skates and had all of them sharpened by the knife man. Then she took them skating.

Last winter, when the village pond had frozen over, Norah had longed for skates. She thought she would be able to do it immediately, but at first she skidded and slipped on the hard cold surface. Soon, though, she was able to take tentative glides, holding Aunt Mary's hand. Gavin clomped around happily, stepping more than skating.

To Norah's surprise, Aunt Mary was really good. Her plump figure became graceful as she turned circles, wove backwards and even performed little jumps. "What fun!" she laughed. "I thought I might have forgotten. Do you know that I once won a cup for skating?" She taught Norah how to keep her balance, and by the end of the afternoon Norah had gone all the way around the rink by herself without falling. The cold air blew by her glowing cheeks as she tried speeding up. It felt like flying.

Then Paige and Bernard appeared and started a game of hockey. When it was over, Norah had fallen so much that her knees, elbows and bottom were sore and wet. But she could hardly wait to skate again the next day.

Gavin turned six at the end of November and Aunt Florence held an elaborate party for him. All the children in his class were invited, as well as the Worsleys and the Smiths. Bernard came too — Gavin had asked for him especially. After a hired magician had performed, the older children helped organize Musical Chairs, Pin the Tail on the Donkey and Button, Button, Who's Got the Button. Then they all sat around the dining-room table for cake and ice cream.

Gavin's face was as bright as his six candles. He had received countless toys and books; the biggest was a red tin fire engine he could ride in. But his favourite present was a tiny sweater for Creature that Hanny had knit on toothpicks. Norah was no longer worried about him being too indulged. Gavin, she decided, was so much himself that no one could spoil him.

After most of the guests had gone home, the Ogilvies, Mr and Mrs Worsley and Norah and Paige collapsed in the living room. Barbara and Daphne had taken over Gavin's Meccano set and were teaching him how to use it in his room.

"Let's have a drink," moaned Aunt Florence. "I'd forgotten how exhausting birthday parties are."

The living room was a disaster: paper hats, burst balloons, streamers and candy wrappers littered the rug. "Shall we start to clean up?" Norah asked.

"The cleaning woman will do it tomorrow," said Aunt Florence with relief.

Norah thought of Gavin's party last year. He'd had only two friends in, but they'd made almost as much mess as thirty children today. It had taken Mum all evening to get the house tidy again.

Today Mum would probably be thinking about Gavin turning six. So would Dad and Grandad and Muriel and Tibby. They would be missing him a lot. She wondered if Mum would make a cake anyway, but that would be difficult this year, with rationing. Norah suddenly wanted to be home so much that she picked up a magazine to hide her brimming eyes.

Paige scratched herself under her pink organdy front. "I wish I could change out of this prickly dress," she whispered to Norah. "I'd like to give it to your friend Dulcie. She kept telling me how much she liked it."

"She can't help it," said Norah automatically. She'd blinked away her tears and was now listening intently to the grown-ups, who were sipping their drinks and talking about the blitz.

"First London and Coventry, now Southampton and Bristol," sighed Mr Worsley. "When will it end?"

"When *will* it?" asked Norah desperately, her voice strained and broken.

He answered carefully. "No one knows, Norah. Not for a long time, I'm afraid." He smiled at her. "It's tough, I know — but we're glad you and Gavin will be here for the duration."

"She's a very brave girl, to endure what she has so far," said Aunt Florence. Every time she said something as flattering as this, Norah was surprised.

Paige chuckled. "Be tough, Norah — endure the duration!"

"Very clever," said her father dryly, "but stop showing off."

Norah sighed. "Endure" and "duration" and "tough" were all hard words — and hard to do. Perhaps now she *could* endure. In the past month she'd "adjusted"; she'd even stopped wetting the bed.

Now she was able to write long, uncensored letters home and say honestly that she was all right. But that still didn't mean she wanted to be here.

XXI

Tidings of Comfort

Norah packed a snowball and threw it at Dulcie's feet. Paige, Barbara and Daphne, in matching tweed coats, tried lying in a row and making snow angels until their mother stopped them. All around the front door of St Peter's Church, children threw polite snowballs that missed their targets or kicked at the ground with impatient feet, unable to play properly in stiff Sunday clothes while surrounded by adults.

Norah edged up to the group that included the two Ogilvies. Maybe if she looked hungry enough, they would get the hint and start for home. Every Sunday Aunt Florence and Aunt Mary talked to the other churchgoers before the service, whispered about them during it and stood around in chattering groups afterwards. It had been the same in Ringden. Grownups seemed to go to church to observe and gossip — and to waste valuable time. Last night it had snowed again. It was almost noon, and Norah still hadn't been set free in it.

"Since this is their first Christmas away from home, we're going to make it as special as possible," Aunt Mary was saying.

"Oh, so are we!" said Mrs Milne eagerly. "We're so worried that Derek and Dulcie and Lucy will be homesick, though they've managed splendidly so far. It's changed our lives, you know, to have children with us."

Aunt Mary said softly, "Yes . . . it's changed ours, too."

Finally the last handshakes were given, the last goodbyes were said and the children were released from waiting. Norah and Gavin ran ahead, kicking up sparkling sprays of snow.

Norah thought about Christmas. No matter how special the Ogilvies tried to make it, she knew Christmas couldn't be the same in Canada. She slowed down, trailing a branch along the sidewalk. While the Ogilvies' household was busy with elaborate Christmas preparations, all she could think of was what her family would be doing at home.

"Will you help me build a snowman after lunch, Norah?" asked Gavin.

Norah nodded. The busier she was, the less time she had to be homesick.

Buying presents was one thing that kept her from brooding. She had helped Hanny pack an enormous food hamper for her family, filled with Christmas pudding, cakes, tins of fruit and fish, and a whole ham. Norah wriggled with excitement as she thought how glad they would be to get it.

"Before you came, the war seemed so far away," said Hanny. "Now it's our war, too."

Aunt Mary had taken them to Woolworth's to buy the rest of their presents. "Hugh and I always did our shopping here when we were your age," she explained. She gave Norah and Gavin a dollar each and left them alone. They spent an hour wandering separately up and down the crowded aisles.

Norah chose a handkerchief for Aunt Mary, "Evening in Paris" perfume for Aunt Florence and a packet of bobby pins for Hanny. Even though Edith was still acting unfriendly, she picked out a purple comb for her. In the toy section she found water pistols for Paige and Bernard and pretend lipstick for Dulcie. Then she remembered Miss Gleeson and got her a bookmark with "This is where I fell asleep" printed on it. Her basket began to be crowded with presents. What a lot of people she knew in Canada!

She couldn't make up her mind about Gavin. He had plenty of cars and planes and soldiers. She turned down the aisle towards the sound of birds, where brightly hued budgies *cheeruped* importantly. Gavin would love one, but they were too expensive. Then she saw a tank of glittering orange goldfish. Five Cents, said the sign. That was perfect.

She found a clerk, who dipped a small net into the tank and scooped out the fish she chose, the brightest and plumpest. He put it with some water into a waxed cardboard carton with a wire handle. She had just enough money left for some food. Norah peeked into the carton and watched the goldfish dart around its temporary home. She would ask Hanny for a jar to use as a bowl and hide it in her wardrobe until Christmas.

When she met Gavin, after paying for her presents first so she could conceal the goldfish in her bag, she discovered he had chosen mothballs for everyone. "It says 'useful' on the package," he explained, sounding out the word carefully. "I like the smell, too."

The next sign of Christmas was a huge party that a wealthy store owner was holding for all the Toronto area war guests. Norah remembered Miss Carmichael telling them about it. She didn't want to feel like an evacuee all over again. "Do I have to go?" she asked.

But Aunt Florence insisted. "And please, Norah, let me buy you a new dress. You'll need one for Christmas dinner anyway, and you simply cannot wear that old Viyella any longer."

"Mum said in her last letter she was cutting down a dress for me out of one of her old ones."

"But it won't get here in time for the party. I want you to look nice — after all, it's a special occasion. And they'll think I'm not taking good care of you if you look shabby."

Norah gave in. "All right," she sighed. Going shopping was a waste of good tobogganing time.

Aunt Florence took her to a fancy store downtown with thick carpets and lots of mirrors. All the salesladies seemed to know who she was. "This way, Mrs Ogilvie," said the lady in charge. "Would you like to sit down?" She took Norah into a changing room and brought dresses in to her.

Norah grew interested in spite of herself. Most of the dresses were too frilly, like the ones Dulcie wore. But there was one she took to immediately. It was red velvet with a simple white collar and cuffs. When she tried it on, the rich weight of it made her feel cosy and secure.

"I like this one," she said, coming out to be inspected. She ran her hands up and down her sides, relishing the thick pile.

"But don't you want to try on the others?"

"No, thank you."

Aunt Florence examined every inch of the dress with the eyes of an experienced shopper. "It certainly looks nice on you — it suits your dark hair." She turned to the woman. "Do you have a hairband that would go with it?"

"Of course, Mrs Ogilvie." The manager bustled away and arrived back breathless with a narrow red band. It matched exactly and made Norah's hair feel neat and out of the way, much more comfortable than awkward bows or scratchy hair-slides.

"Very well, we'll take it. You have good taste, my dear. Now shoes."

Aunt Florence bought Norah black patent strapped shoes and new white socks. Norah peeked at the bill when it was all rung up and gulped. Even in pounds, it was an enormous sum.

"This is awfully expensive, Aunt Florence."

"Nonsense. It's nice to have someone to spend money on."

Norah swallowed her pride and said thank you.

"Oh, Norah, just look at these!" cried Aunt Florence. She held up a pair of red velvet shorts. "Aren't they wonderful? Gavin would look adorable in them and then you'd match. I'll take a pair in size six."

When they got home Gavin took one look at the shorts and shook his head. "I don't like them. Thank you, anyway," he added, politely but firmly.

Aunt Florence was surprised; it was the first time Gavin had rebelled. "Well, maybe they *are* too young for you," she conceded. "I'll return them and you can wear your sailor suit to the party."

Gavin smiled. He liked his sailor suit because it had a whistle.

Aunt Mary dropped them off at the Royal York Hotel, where the party was being held. It was the same towering building where Norah and Gavin had sheltered on the day they ran away; Aunt Mary told them it was the largest hotel in the Empire. A woman conducted them into a huge ballroom milling with dressed-up children. Norah held Gavin's hand as they stood amidst the shrill voices.

"Why, it's Norah and Gavin!" Miss Carmichael rushed up and kissed them. "Don't you both look well! You've put on weight — our Canadian food must be agreeing with you. What a lovely dress, Norah! Are you all settled in now? Do you like your school?"

"Yes, thank you." Norah answered all her questions politely and Gavin began to tell her about grade one. Miss Carmichael was *kind*, Norah realized. She had been kind at the residence too, but Norah had been too miserable to notice. That confusing week seemed a long time ago.

"You're losing some of your accent, Gavin," said Miss Carmichael. "By the time you go back to England you'll sound like a Canadian! Yours is changing too, Norah."

Surely it wasn't. Norah didn't want to lose her accent. It wasn't fair that it could happen without her consent.

Dulcie and Lucy found them and they all made their way to the food. "Derek wouldn't come," said Dulcie. "He says he's too old for a children's party and that he's a Canadian now, not a war guest. I love your dress, Norah."

Norah was confused. She didn't want to be a Canadian *or* a war guest; she just wanted to be herself. But the long tables of food distracted her. They were piled with Christmas cake, punch, cookies and dishes of candy. Norah had to stop Gavin from stuffing his pockets. She recognized some children from the SS *Zandvoort* and they stood in a circle and compared their new families.

"We have a dog!" boasted Johnnie.

"I live with my aunt and uncle in a small town outside Toronto," said Margery. "I have my own chickens and I sell the eggs."

For a second Norah envied her; it would have been nice to have been sent somewhere that was more like home. But then she wouldn't be with the Ogilvies. That would seem strange, she was so used to them now.

Seeing some of the children from the ship made her wonder how Jamie was; she'd forgotten all about him.

"Aren't you excited about Christmas, Norah?" Dulcie asked her. "We're going to a pantomime at the Royal Alexandra Theatre. Aunt Dorothy is going to ask you, too." Norah didn't want to disillusion Dulcie by telling her that Canadian Christmas wasn't going to be the same.

A man called for silence and introduced their host. Everyone cheered and clapped and one of the older British girls gave a short speech of thanks. "We are all touched and grateful at how the Canadians have welcomed us into their homes," she said. "Let's show our appreciation, everyone."

There was more clapping and one of the adults began to sing "There'll always be an England." Norah groaned, but halfway through the song she joined in. Everything at this party was as it had been at the beginning: all of them crowded into a room with speeches and singing. But it didn't bother her any more; somehow it didn't seem important enough to worry about.

"It wasn't too bad," she admitted to Aunt Florence on the way home. But she was glad it was over.

"It was super!" said Gavin through a mouthful of fudge. "I'm glad we're war guests."

"I'm not!" blurted out Norah, forgetting to be grateful.

Aunt Florence glanced at her. "Sending you away must have been a terrible decision for your parents to make. But since they did, I'm happy it was our home you came to."

At school everyone was getting so excited about the holidays that for the first time Miss Liers had trouble keeping order. She tried to get them to sing a carol every morning, but they kept changing the words to "While shepherds washed their socks by night" and "Good King Wenceslas looked out/In his pink pyjamas."

"That's enough! We won't have *any* singing, if you're going to act so silly!" She slammed down the piano lid. Norah shared in the suppressed giggles of the class. Poor Miss Liers — she never seemed to want to have any fun.

One afternoon, when Norah went as usual to pick up Gavin at his classroom, some other British children were standing around the grade one and two cloakroom, looking doleful. Lucy was crying and Dulcie was trying to comfort her. "We didn't get the *presents* . . . " she wailed.

"What happened?" Norah asked. Gavin and Lucy tried to explain.

After lunch a film crew had arrived at Prince Edward School to make a movie of all the kindergarten to grade two war guests. They were going to send it to England so their parents could see their children having a happy Christmas in Canada.

"He took us into the gym and there was a huge Christmas tree," sniffed Lucy. "There were all sorts of presents underneath."

"The man said they were just empty boxes," said Gavin solemnly. "He said we had to open them and pretend they were presents, because it was just a game for the movie."

"But they weren't empty at all!" said Lucy. "There were dolls and games and I got a music box that played 'Somewhere over the Rainbow'." She began to cry again. "But at the end of the movie we had to give them back. He said all the toys belonged to his children!"

"Never mind," said Dulcie. "Soon it will really be Christmas and you'll have presents you can keep."

Norah wondered if her parents would see the movie. She had never known that being evacuees would involve so much attention — applauding crowds, newspaper photographs, broadcasts from the princesses and now a movie.

The next week there was another radio message, one far more personal than the one from Princess Elizabeth. "I have a wonderful surprise for you, Norah and Gavin," bubbled Aunt Mary. "The CBC is sending messages to Canada from your parents. They can't give us an exact time, but after school today you might hear their voices!"

Norah couldn't believe it, not until they all crowded around the radio that afternoon. Out of the shiny wooden case came faint British voices, full of longing: "Keep your chin up, Tim . . . We miss you, Kathleen and David . . . Happy Christmas, Margaret . . . " Before each message, the announcer said the family's name.

As the broadcast went on, Norah's throat constricted with fear. She thought of her terrible dream. Ever since she'd had it, she had waited even more avidly than before for letters from her family to make sure that they were all right. But she hadn't had one for two weeks. If she didn't hear her parents' voices now, the worst might have happened.

But then the announcer said, "And now we have a message for Norah and Gavin Stoakes, who are staying with the Ogilvies in Toronto."

Mum's light voice filled the quiet room. "Hello, Norah and Gavin. We want you to know that we miss you and love you." She wavered at the end.

"Dad here. Have a very happy Christmas. Everyone is fine and Grandad and the girls send their love."

That was all.

Gavin had frozen as soon as he heard his mother. When the message was over his mouth hung open for a second; then he began to babble. "That was Muv and Dad! Did you hear that, Norah? Did you, Aunt Florence? That was my *muv!*" He looked at Aunt Florence doubtfully and pulled Creature out of his pocket. On his face was the same bewildered expression he'd had when he first left home.

"You poor little boy . . . " began Aunt Mary, but her mother gave her a sharp glance.

"I did hear them, Gavin," she said. "Didn't they sound close? Now you come with me and we'll have a nice story about Pooh." She led him out of the room.

They had sounded *too* close, thought Norah. It made it all the harder to accept that they were so far away. How could their voices come all the way across the ocean? She wondered where they'd gone to send their messages — to London? Mum would have got all dressed up in her grey suit and Dad would pretend he wasn't nervous. And Grandad would bluster about being left behind.

"O-oh tidings of co-omfort and joy," sang a choir at the end of the broadcast. It *had* been a kind of comfort, to hear their familiar voices. At least she knew they were safe. But it wasn't a joy. She would only feel joy if she could be with them for Christmas.

"Are you all right, Norah?" asked Aunt Mary. She took out the cribbage board. "Shall we have a game?"

Norah was good at cribbage now. She let herself think only of her peg drawing ahead of Aunt Mary's.

On Christmas Eve afternoon Norah helped Aunt Mary balance Christmas cards on top of picture frames. They were waiting for the "Drummond clan," as Aunt Florence called it, to arrive; some of the Montreal cousins were driving down to stay for three days. Edith had spent the whole morning complaining and making up beds in the spare rooms. Three great-nieces were to sleep on cots and the extra bed in Norah's tower. She tried not to worry about what they would be like.

She had never seen so many cards. At home her parents got just enough to fill the mantlepiece, but dozens and dozens had arrived at the Ogilvies.

"You must know a lot of people," she said to Aunt Mary.

"Well, the Drummonds and Ogilvies are both very large families and since Mother is the oldest, all the friends of the family send cards to her. We're never able to get them all up. And the trouble with getting so many is the number we have to send."

Norah had seen Aunt Florence's special notebook, with long lists of names and ticks for sending and receiving cards. Some names got crossed off, and some added; it was like an elaborate game.

She had received five Christmas cards herself. There was one from her principal and joint ones to her and Gavin from Joey's mother and Mrs Curteis. Another was from Molly. She said she was sorry Norah had been evacuated too, but she hoped she was having a good time in Canada. "Wales is very wet," she wrote. "Sometimes I get homesick, but Mother and Dad are coming here for Christmas."

The last card had an English robin on the front. It said:

Dear Norah,
The dogfights have stopped so I guess the Battle of Britain is over. Now there are bombs in London instead. We don't have the Skywatchers any more. I have the most shrapnel in the village. When are you coming back?

Your friend,
Tom

Both of these cards were so unsettling that Norah put them on her windowsill without reading them again. Molly and Tom and her other friends at home seemed like people in another life.

"There!" Aunt Mary stepped down from her stool.

"I think we're finally ready."

Norah followed her glance around the living room. Every picture had cards stuck on top and large bunches of holly stood in silver bowls on the tables. In one corner was the largest Christmas tree Norah had ever seen, making the room smell like a forest.

"Turn the lights on, Norah," said Aunt Mary. "They should be here any moment. I'll go and help Hanny get things ready."

Norah plugged in the tree. She and Gavin had helped decorate it with fragile glass balls, crocheted snowflakes and lights that bubbled. As the lights heated up, the balls swayed gently. On the top branch perched an angel with gauzy wings.

It was certainly a beautiful tree . . . but Norah thought of another one, the little tree that Dad cut down in Stumble Wood each year and set on a table in the front room. There were no strings of lights, but the tinsel on it sparkled in the light coming through the window. She remembered making paper chains; opening a new package of coloured paper that sometimes included a few silver or even gold strips and the whole family sitting around the kitchen table pasting the strips into circles. They hung the chains in garlands from corner to corner in all the rooms; Dad's head would brush against them. Last of all they hung the mistletoe from the front door and everyone who visited was trapped under it and kissed, accompanied by shrieks of laughter . . .

Norah blinked hard and looked at the Ogilvies' tree again. Presents were piled so high under it that its lower branches were hidden. More were beside it against the wall. Many of the presents had her and Gavin's names on them. One large parcel was wrapped in brown paper and string. It looked plain beside the fancy paper of the rest, but it said "To Norah from Mum and Dad". She was going to open that one first.

A faint stirring of excitement rose in Norah. She bent to rattle her parents' present. Then the door knocker sounded and she quickly dropped the parcel.

"Merry Christmas!" cried voices in the hall. "Aunt Florence! Aunt Mary! And who's this cute kid? You must be Gavin."

A crowd of people swarmed into the living room, bearing even more presents. Norah stepped back as they kept pouring in. All of them had loud ringing voices and a purposeful bearing. A whole roomful of people related to the Ogilvies was too much to take in.

"And this is Norah, our other war guest," said Aunt Florence. She looked proud and put her arm across Norah's shoulder as she introduced her. Norah drew strength from its warmth as she said "How do you do" again and again.

After they had all sat down with their drinks, she began to sort them out. There were five adults and five children. Two little boys about Gavin's age would be sleeping in his room.

The three girls brought their ginger ale over to sit beside Norah. The eldest was Florence — Flo, she corrected quickly. She was fourteen and her sister Janet was eleven. The other girl, Clare, was twelve. They chatted with an assurance that made Norah feel like a stranger again. After all, they were really family, not just guests.

Janet looked the nicest of the girls; she had a plain, broad face and laughed a lot. "I'm so excited, I think I might be sick!" she told Norah. "I usually am at Christmas."

"Please spare us this year," said Flo. She tossed back her long hair, looking sophisticated. Clare was complaining about having to come. "We have to every year," she explained. "It's a tradition. But I wanted to go skiing with my friends in Montreal."

Beside her, her mother gave her a warning look and began to ask Norah the usual questions. "I bet you get tired of telling people how you like Canada," whispered Janet. Norah grinned and moved closer to her on the chesterfield.

"Have you been to Gairloch yet?" asked Janet.

"Oh, yes!" said Norah eagerly. She had forgotten about Gairloch. "I liked it there."

"Wait till you see it in the summer! It's my favourite place in the whole world. We have lots of fun sleeping over the boathouse. We sneak out at night and go skinny dipping, and catch frogs and put them in the Boys' Dorm."

All of this sounded scary but intriguing. Norah recalled the peace of the rippling lake, the screen of trees and the friendly old cottage. Next summer she would be able to spend three months there. Next summer . . .

Gavin and the two younger cousins seemed to have turned into one very noisy boy, racing cars up and down the hall floor. "Quiet, you three!" called a mother. "Go and wash your hands for dinner."

The clan trooped into the dining-room. Dinner was modest in anticipation of tomorrow's feast: tourtière and salad. Before dessert, Norah jumped as everyone started chanting at once: "*You* scream, *I* scream, we *all* scream for ice cream!" Hanny marched in with a glass bowlful of it.

Norah ate hers silently, feeling left out again. What other strange rituals did this family have?

After dinner they stood around the piano and sang carols while an uncle played. Then Aunt Florence read part of *A Christmas Carol* aloud. By now the little boys were nodding. All seven children, despite Flo's protests, were sent to get ready for bed.

At home Norah laid one of Dad's socks across the end of her bed, but here they hung specially knitted, patterned stockings on hooks under the mantel. Aunt Mary had found hers and Hugh's for Norah and Gavin, and the cousins brought their own. Gavin had stopped saying "Father Christmas" ever since he'd been taken to the Santa Claus parade in November. Aunt Florence let him be the one to put out the milk and cookies on the hearth.

"Now off to bed!" she smiled. "Santa won't come until you're asleep."

"Will he find me here?" asked Gavin anxiously. "Will he think I'm still in England?"

Aunt Florence kissed him. "He'll find you — I told him where you were." Gavin stared at her with awe, then went up with the others to bed.

Flo and Janet and Clare talked and laughed and tossed on their narrow beds for a long time. At first Norah didn't like sharing her room with three strangers, especially when they told her they always slept up here at Christmas. She wanted to let them know it was *her* room now, but she couldn't find the right words.

"How can you bear living with Aunt Florence?" asked Flo. "She's so bossy, she thinks she's the Queen!" Flo got up, stuffed her pillow under the top of her nightgown and tied it in place with a belt. Then she sauntered across the room, bowing left and right. "You may kiss my hand," she said haughtily.

For a second Norah was shocked. Then she laughed so hard they had to pat her on the back. How wonderful to be able to be so wicked, to make fun of Aunt Florence with someone else who knew her! Norah began to talk as easily with the cousins as if she were really related to them. She fell asleep in the middle of telling a joke.

Something in the room made Norah stir. She turned over and felt a weight on her feet.

Of course — her filled stocking. Aunt Florence or Aunt Mary — or Santa Claus, she smiled — must have crept in and put it there. It felt exactly the same as her stocking at home. It was one of the most familiar feelings she knew, but she always forgot about it until Christmas. Every year, for as long as she could remember, she had woken up in the early morning dimness and felt that delectable weight on her feet. She never let herself touch it until it was really morning; she always fell back immediately to sleep.

But now she lay awake. The thrill of the stocking was the same — but nothing else was. It never would be again. She was far away from her own family in a strange country, and she would probably be here for a long time.

But she had ways to get through it. A family she was finally feeling a part of, with a new, unexpected set of "cousins". And Paige's family, and Bernard's. Perhaps it took three borrowed families to make up for one real one. There was Gairloch to look forward to in the summer. And most important of all, Gavin to take care of.

Gavin's goldfish! Norah slipped out of bed and padded to her wardrobe, trying not to wake the others. The goldfish was swimming friskily around its bowl. She picked it up carefully. She would take it down to Gavin's room and put it where he'd see it first thing in the morning.

Norah tiptoed down the stairs and into his room. At first she couldn't find him amidst the visitors. He was slumbering peacefully, Creature by his cheek. She placed the bowl on the table beside his bed and slipped under it the card she had prepared: "A very Happy Christmas to Gavin from Norah." She watched his face for a few seconds. Whatever else happened during their time in Canada, she was going to make sure Gavin kept on being as happy as he could be.

She was still wide awake. It was exciting to be the only one in the slumbering household. She decided to sneak down and peek at the tree again. The living room was dark and chilly, but after she plugged in the tree it came alive. In the darkness the lights glowed even more gloriously than they had in the daytime. Norah stood in front of the tree with her hands out, watching them change colour.

Then she gasped. Propped against a chair by the tree was a shiny new bicycle. Holding her breath with suspense, she read the card tied to its handlebars: "Merry Christmas to Norah with love from Aunt Florence."

It was a Hurricane, like Paige's — maroon with gold striping. It even had a dynamo set and a large wicker basket. She ran her hands over the smooth chrome and the leather seat, not quite sure whether to believe it was real. When they played horses, she would *call* it "Hurricane", to remind her of the planes.

A bicycle meant freedom. It meant Aunt Florence trusted her and knew her well enough to guess what she wanted the most. Norah longed to climb onto it, to continue to caress it; but she shouldn't be here, seeing her present before morning. Quickly she unplugged the tree and fled up to bed. She shivered and squirmed under the covers to get warm again, giggling to herself. A bicycle!

Someone crunched by in the snowy street outside. A man and woman's voices sang softly as they passed: "Where the snow lay round about / Deep and crisp and even."

Norah sat up and pulled the curtains open. She was suddenly filled to the brim with Christmas, with the magic feeling that came every year. Christmas was the same, after all. If Christmas carried on in Canada as it did at home, maybe other good things would stay the same as well.

Norah bounced down again into her cosy bed, making the bell on her stocking jingle. She lay on her back and watched the dim, pewter-coloured clouds outside. Her breathing was light and easy, as if a heavy weight had rolled away. All that fell out of the sky was soft white snow.

Afterword

During World War II around 15,000 British children were evacuated overseas. Nearly 8,000 of them came to Canada; most were privately sponsored but 1,500 were assisted by the Children's Overseas Reception Board. Of these government-sponsored children about one third, like Norah and Gavin, went to the homes of complete strangers.

The response of Canadians to the plight of British children was overwhelming; probably many more children would have been brought over if the tragic sinking of *The City of Benares* had not brought an end to evacuation plans. A fascinating account of Canada's involvement is given in the late Geoffrey Bilson's *The Guest Children*, the only non-fiction book so far devoted entirely to the subject.

My book, however, is fiction. There is no doubt that many of the children who came to Canada enjoyed

the adventure and found warm, welcoming homes.
I tried to imagine a child who didn't. My depiction of
the events of the war is as true as possible for someone
who was born just after it. The major places, too, are
real. But most of the details, such as Norah's village, the
ship, her school, her local library and, especially, the
characters, are fictional creations.

I would not have been able to write this story
without the help of many people. Thank you to Bryan
Bacon; Auriol Hastie; Jacquetta, Shaun and the late Pat
Jackson; Kay and Sandy Pearson; Kathleen Tankard;
and Alan Woodland for sharing with me their ex-
periences of the war; to David Conn for his invaluable
advice about the Battle of Britain; to Sarah Ellis and Jean
Little for reading the manuscript; to Patrick Dunn for
procuring books from all over the continent; to David
Kilgour for his sleuthing; and to Vicki Lazier and
Christine McMeans for remembering a family song.
Above all I would like to thank Alice Kane, from whom
I first heard "Alenoushka and her Brother", and whose
story of telling it to evacuated children inspired this
book.

FIC
PEA

        Pearson, Kit

    The Sky is Falling

Sandy School Library
Sandy, OR 97055

DEMCO

Sandy School Library
Sandy, OR 97055